COFFEE SPOONS

and

OTHER STORIES

by

Susan O'Byrne

Timshel Press, 2018

Coffee Spoons and Other Stories

Printed in the United States of America

First printing, 2018

ISBN 978-1985345454

Timshel Press

Hinsdale, IL 60521

For my Dad, who waited a long time for this, and my Mom, who always shares her books.

TABLE OF CONTENTS

1. Pick A Little

September's Book Club meeting was comic gold, just as Denise had suspected. Lynette hosted, which meant that all seven ladies were crammed into her spartan, but tasteful, sitting room off the foyer, where they perched on high-backed mission style chairs that didn't really allow one to slouch or relax. Well, six of them had so perched; Jackie, late as usual, had no chair at all. Before Lynette could retrieve an extra chair from the dining room, Jackie had plopped herself on the ottoman and crossed her legs, eyes gleaming in anticipation. Jackie treated every book club meeting like a full-contact competitive sport.

Lynette's fourteen year-old neurotic Maltese Terrier, Peanut, whined and paced from the foyer to the dining room, where the ladies had laid out the evening's treats. At least, the crazy dog had been mostly trained to not get into their faces when they were visiting, Denise noted to herself. And Peanut (or "Pea-Pea," as Lynette rather bizarrely called him, to the girls' inevitable shrieks of laughter) was too tiny and arthritic to reach anything.

The rule was: bring a bottle of wine or a treat. They tried to coordinate, lest the unlikely scenario of no treats should occur (there was never any danger of someone forgetting to bring wine in this group). Tonight, there was a plate of turtle brownies, a bowl of homemade guacamole and tortilla chips, warm bacon gorgonzola dip, and a package of Chips Ahoy. The latter item had been placed laughingly on the table by Sandra.

"Long day, ladies," she announced. "Grabbed this from the pantry on my way out. Where's the wine?"

The club was a bit of a neighborhood institution. Cathy Wilson, along with Denise and Lauren, had founded it over ten years ago. The three women were neighbors, living within a few blocks of each other on or near Chester Street. The three had seen each other around town over the years, but hadn't connected until each had a Kindergartner enrolled at Washington Elementary in the fall of 2009. The school was only a few blocks' walk away; Cathy had met Denise and Lauren as she chased after little Erin, who was madly racing down the sidewalk on her scooter. Cathy, wearing an orthopedic boot after breaking her right big toe, hobbled after Erin, shrieking, "Stop at the corner! Stop at the corner!" The two other women, also walking their own children to Washington, immediately sensed potential disaster and sprang into action. Lauren pushed her daughter over to Denise and ran ahead to corral the errant child. Denise held the hand of Lauren's daughter and introduced her to little Zack. Cathy lurched closer, swearing under her breath.

"This is not what I envisioned for her first day of school," she panted.

"Hi there, I'm Denise Monarch," Denise reached out her hand.

"And obviously I'm Mother of The Year," Cathy replied, and the two burst into laughter.

"Whoa down there, sweetie!" Lauren called, stepping in front of Erin as she scooted. The child was slight and yellow-haired, wearing a pale pink tee shirt with a ballerina-cat on it. She blinked curiously at Lauren, then turned her scooter around and headed back to her mother.

2

Over the decade of their more or less regular monthly meetings, they had read 112 books, from Stephen King to John Irving to Nora Roberts. Truth be told, there was not a huge amount of literary discussion. The women came together as young mothers. Some were new to Whistler and in need of a social outlet. Some had lived there all their lives, and simply liked meeting new people. A few had joined because they thought being in a book club might help their standing in the community. Those ladies had not stayed long; it wasn't that kind of book club.

To reserve books at the Whistler Public Library, their group needed a name; it was Denise who suggested they call themselves the "Mothers of the Year." It was not as regimented as many clubs; they did not meet every month on a set date. Sometimes, only one or two of the women admitted to even having read the book. They were a laissez-faire operation.

Over the past decade, they had laughed and cried each other through the loss of parents (Heather's dad and Lynette's stepmother), the loss of marriage (Lauren's), and the loss of their children's virginity (Cathy's older son, Jack, who fashioned himself a poet and had memorialized the momentous event in sonnet form – now *that* had been a book club meeting for the record books). The Mothers had seen at least eight women come and go from the club for various reasons: Nicole and Greta's families had moved away; Whitney, Joanne and Deirdre confessed they just didn't want to keep up with the reading load. The others had simply drifted off without any explanation.

Jackie was an odd addition to their club. Her family had moved in across the street from Heather last spring. Heather walked over her customary Welcome batch of Rice Krispy treats and met Michael, Jackie's husband, as he organized rakes and tool kits in the garage. He was small and dark, with narrow shoulders and a five o'clock shadow.

"I can't get over all the space we have," Michael had said. It's unbelievable having storage space to spare. You've got to understand: we moved here from Brooklyn. I was at Costco yesterday; it was like a stadium!"

His candor won Heather over immediately. She learned Michael and Jackie had a pair of twins, Dashiell and Hayes, and that Michael had been promoted and transferred, uprooted with his family to Whistler.

"My company is in the city," Michael explained. "But we wanted Whistler for the schools. Jackie insisted on a town with excellent school districts." Michael went on to explain his wife's bookishness. Jackie had worked as a Development Editor at W.W. Norton Publishing Company in New York prior to having the twins.

In an overabundance of neighborliness, Heather urged Michael to have Jackie join the book club: "She'll be a wonderful addition, and she'll meet all sorts of women from the neighborhood."

Though she was in her mid-forties, Jackie hadn't married till her later-thirties, so Dashiell and Hayes were still toddlers. By contrast, the children of the other members were all at least in middle school by now, and Denise's oldest boy, Ted, was already in college.

"She's having a heckuva time with those twins," Heather told the others. "Her husband said it's been rough. I'm glad she's going to join our little gang."

"Aw, we'll make her feel right at home, won't we girls?" Sandra said.

But Jackie was not the type to feel right at home; she was brooding and appeared ill at ease until after a glass or two of wine. Then, however, her tongue became too loosened and she shocked the Mothers of the Year with her blistering literary commentary.

To Jackie, anything west of Philadelphia was a cultural wasteland. She had worked in Publishing. She had regularly attended edgy off-Broadway plays, not the splashy big ticket musicals that the tourists flocked to (and the Book Club ladies enjoyed). She missed the Met and the MOMA and the "energy" of her former home. She was used to walking across the Brooklyn Bridge. She couldn't understand why you couldn't get a decent curry in Whistler. She was baffled by what she called the "freaky whiteness" of Whistler's demographics. She never had imagined she would become, Jackie told them (with just the faintest touch of a grimace), a stay-at-home mother.

As a general rule, Jackie despised most of their reading choices, deploring them for being "manipulative," "sentimental," or, less prosaically, "crap." Jackie's entry radically changed the genial chemistry of the club; Jackie felt compelled to improve everyone's mind, which was a sweet gesture, Denise thought, if misplaced. None of the members fully understood why she bothered to keep attending each month.

They had gotten off to an awkward start with Jackie back last summer. They'd all met at Cathy's house to discuss *Where'd You Go, Bernadette*; Jackie had arrived with Heather, a bottle of Kim Crawford Sauvignon Blanc in her tote bag.

"So, everyone, this is Jackie Bloom! She just moved her from New York." Heather gushed.

There were handshakes, cheek kisses and general pleasantries exchanged. Sandra frowned a bit and pursed her lips. "Oh, gosh, you look like someone, but I can't put my finger on it. Can any of you girls tell who?"

Jackie demurred. "Oh, I get that all the time. Natalie Portman in *Black Swan*. I used to get stopped by people on the subway all the time when it came out."

Sandra, who realized she had been thinking that Jackie resembled the actress who played the mom in the *Diary of a Wimpy Kid* movies, simply nodded and smiled politely.

Heather speculated that Jackie, whose twins were rejecting her increasingly frantic efforts to potty train them, was starved for social time with other adults, so even though she hated their book choices, she felt compelled to attend. Lauren, less kind-hearted than Heather, suggested Jackie merely wanted an excuse to drink and shoot off her mouth.

5

Tonight's book was *Me Before You*, by JoJo Moyes.

"Let's go over our scores now," said Lynette, getting out an iPad. The club rated their selections on a scale of one through five. "I'll start. I give it a five. I couldn't stop crying at the end. What did you think?" she gestured to Sandra on her right.

"Five. Loved it!"

"Four"

"Four"

"Sorry, didn't finish."

Three and a half."

And then Jackie: "Can I give it zero stars? No? Ok, one. That book was abysmal. It was the worst kind of pandering and talk down to a female audience. It was the classic Cinderella myth, only the Prince is in a wheelchair. He dies so she can live; absolute manipulative crap" Jackie got up from the ottoman, poured herself another glass of Seven Deadly Zins, and then continued to decry the novel's plausibility and characterization.

Lauren ignored her. "They're making a movie of it, I heard. Why don't we all go as a group?"

After a few more glasses of wine, Lynette and Heather engaging in a weepy discussion on the novel's theme of assisted suicide.

"No, it's not like I think it's the right thing to do," Lynette sniffled. "It's just I totally understand why he would want to die like that. With dignity."

"And what would you say to the tens of thousands of quadriplegics in the world, who are trying so hard to have any voice at all? This author, 'JoJo' seems to think they are better off not living than not functioning perfectly." snapped Jackie. "That's bullshit."

"She's not telling people what to do; that's what the character wanted to do," said Lauren.

"Well, who do you think created the character?"

There was a small silence. Peanut started yipping mysteriously at something (or nothing) outside the front door. Then Sandra piped up, "Did anyone else get water in their

6

basement last week with that bad rain? As usual, we got some moisture coming in from the window well. Such a pain in the butt."

And the rest of the evening's conversations then shifted completely away from assisted suicide and onto cheerleading (had they heard about how Carla's girl, Aimee, had torn her meniscus?) and SAT test prepping ("highway robbery, courtesy of Kaplan") and braces (Lauren asked the group to remind her to become an orthodontist in her next life). The conversation, freed from the awkward shackles of literary analysis, grew louder.

Peanut entered the room with the delicate, stiff gait of elderly pets. He sniffed at each lady in turn, hoping for a cookie handout or cheese square until Lynnette ordered him out and he stared at their congregation morosely, his damp muzzle resting on his paws.

"Poor little Pea-Pea," Denise snickered.

"Not getting' anything tonight, are you, darlin'?" added Lauren. And the two women roared.

At the end, they all rather boozily hugged and exchanged well wishes, setting the next Book Club meeting for November 10th at Sandra's house. She had chosen *Go Set a Watchman*, the new book by Harper Lee.

"At least I know you'll like it because it's by the *To Kill a Mockingbird* lady!" Sandra said to Jackie. "It's a classic."

It was about ten by the time Denise arrived back home. They'd had to call it a night early because two of the gals had high schoolers rowing on crew team, and had to be ready by 6:15 on Saturday morning.

It was only about three-quarters of a mile from Lynette's house on Larch to Denise's home on North Parkside Street. Whistler in general was filled with homes that local realtors described as "stately" and "elegant;" the families on Parkside Street did not boast coach houses or swimming pools in their backyards, like the folks on the tonier South Side of town. These homes were merely lovely and comfortable, not extravagant.

Instead of the CEOs and Professional Baseball players who lived in the sprawling estates of the South side, families like the Monarchs were occupied largely by attorneys, physicians and financial planners. They could not properly be designated the mega-rich themselves, but the families on Parkside Street were well within spitting distance.

The Monarch's house had a brick and cedar exterior and neat white shutters around the windows that faced the street. Jason and Denise had lived there since their oldest child, Ted, was a baby. Jason was, not surprisingly for a Friday night, lying on his back on the sofa with the television on.

"Back so soon?" he asked. Jason Monarch was 52; his dark brown hair had long since retreated from his forehead. He was Vice-President of Finance at Summit5 in the city.

"Mackinley and Charlotte both have crew in the morning, so Cathy and Lynette have to get up at the crack of dawn. We didn't want to overstay our welcome." Denise replied.

"Any good stories?"

"Well, that New York Jackie got all drunk and belligerent again, but that's hardly news."

Jason laughed. "You wanna keep the party going? I can open up a bottle?" He was looking for an excuse, of course. The Monarchs had a fairly impressive collection of Bordeaux in the wine fridge downstairs.

"Have at it, my dear." Denise took off her boots. Why did she wear boots? She hated them; they made her feet sweat so terribly. But they were axiomatic in Whistler in the fall. "What's up with the kids?"

"Mia is at her friend whatshername's down the street, and Zack is in the basement." Teddy, of course, was up at school; they wouldn't see him till Parents' Weekend in a couple weeks.

Zack, who no longer remembered the scooter chase from his first day of Kindergarten, was now fifteen, taller than Denise, and lunging close to Jason's height. His voice was improbably low for someone so skinny. His hands and feet seemed like the oversized paws on a Labrador puppy. Zack vacillated between being a sullen teen and a goofy teen, and was therefore basically a normal teen. His grades were middling to good, so Denise didn't hassle him too much about the hours he spent gaming (or "farting around with that stupid thing," as Denise occasionally put it) on the Xbox in the basement.

Zack missed his big brother quite a bit. The two had become closer in the past few years, after Ted had gone through a bad spell that affected his grades, and worse, his emotional well-being. Jason and Denise had been worried sick about their oldest child, who wasn't sleeping or eating enough, and looked frankly terrible. He was seeing a counsellor, but even after six weeks, Denise couldn't find any visible improvement in poor Teddy's demeanor. Miraculously, Zack suddenly started badgering Ted to help him improve his basketball skills. Teddy played for the Whistler High School Wolverines. Having a project, working on something he was good at and confident in, helped to start Ted out of his funk. It was clear that Zack would never play for the NBA and probably would not even make the high school team, but the sight of her two boys (one so thin and haunted, the other trying so hard to be like his brother) out playing "horse" in the driveway made Denise's eyes fill with proud tears. Now that Ted was away at school, Zack was more subdued, but the boys frequently texted and facetimed each other. They'd be seeing Teddy soon, thank goodness. She missed him more than she wanted to admit.

Mia, twelve, was in middle school. She would be fine, once her body and hormones stopped rebelling against her. With poor Mia, one didn't know from one day to the next whether she would be crying tears of anguish from hating all her friends, desperately need or reject her mother, or remember basics of hygiene, like brushing her teeth or hair.

Mia's latest episode of high drama had been the spectacular break-up and reconciliation of her friendship with Ellie Newman. The two had been together since they were enrolled in pre-ballet class together at three years old. They'd made it through the collectible Japanese eraser phase, the slime creation madness, the fidget spinner craze, and the rainbow unicorn llama sloth trend. The real tension began, however, with the onset of the first middle school crush phase. Both girls had their eyes on Aiden MacPherson, a nice enough kid, with enviable eyelashes. Aiden told his friend Josh that he liked Mia, and Josh subsequently told most of the Seventh Grade class, which means the entire universe to a twelve year-old girl. Ellie was heartbroken; Mia was mortified; poor Aiden was simply confused. Ellie told Mia she had to "choose between" her and Aiden. Denise's understanding of the story got a bit confused after this point, but the upshot for now at least appeared to be that Mia believed that friendships trump boys. Which, in Denise's humble opinion, was extraordinarily wise.

"What do you say to a nice Pauillac?" Jason called from the basement.

"Great." Denise went upstairs to change out of her tunic and tights into the mom-uniform of yoga pants and a drapey tee-shirt.

"I did pick up a nice tidbit of gossip," Denise offered. "Maria Schroeder, do you remember her? She got her boobs done and had a big boob-reveal party!"

"This is why you need to socialize more," Jason said. "Why don't we ever get invited to those kind of parties?"

Denise rolled her eyes. "Don't you think that's absolutely wacko? A boob-reveal party – to show off the new pair she just bought?"

"Indeed not. I fully support such an endeavor." Jason quipped.

"Oh, before I forget," Denise was looking at her phone. "John Bolger has two tickets for the game on Sunday. They can't go and wanted to know if you and Zack are interested."

"Do I know a John Bolger?"

"Heather's husband? Urologist? Glasses?" Denise hinted.

"Doctor John!" Jason cried in recognition. "He's a good guy. Are they good seats?"

"How would I know?" Denise asked. "I doubt they're nosebleeds, at least."

"I think Zack would have a blast. Let's do it!" Jason nodded.

"Just so you know, the game is at noon. You'll have to give yourselves at least an hour to get into the city. No Sunday sleeping in." Denise reminded him.

"Shit, game's off." Jason replied, then laughed. It was a running joke between Jason and Denise that Jason held his ability to sleep in on weekends in solemn reverence. For Denise, who always rose at six o'clock regardless of the day, this behavior was a nearly constant source of irritation, especially when the kids required chauffeuring to various weekend activities at any time before ten-thirty. For football, Jason would make an exception. That the forecast for this weekend was warm and sunny doubtless helped as well.

"So, let me tell you about tonight," said Denise, as she refilled her glass of Bordeaux. "The book was moronic, but who cares, right? It was one of those dime a dozen weepers and a couple girls got all wound-up about it and teary-eyed. But Jackie starts in going Full Professor on everyone. Nobody gives a shit what she thinks, but the gal wouldn't shut up. Finally, Sandra just changed the subject and we could all breathe a sigh of relief."

"Remind me again why you wanted this woman in the group?" Jason asked.

Denise rolled her eyes. "Heather thought the husband was cute, so she brought it up to him when they met."

"And *men* get the bad rap?"

The front door creaked open and Mia walked in. Ellie and her father, Matt, called out "Goodnight!" from the porch, then turned to walk back home. They lived roughly two blocks away.

"Hey, Princess, how was it at Ellie's?" Denise inquired.

Mia sighed theatrically, "Oh, it was alright. Except for her little sisters. They're horrible! They kept *interrupting* us while we were *trying* to watch *The Hunger Games*. It was *tortuous*." She flounced upstairs.

Jason looked at Denise with a smile, "Tortuous. At least she's got a good vocabulary."

"I *heard* that! Do you think I'm *deaf*?"

"Get ready for bed, honey. It's after ten." Denise called out. "Come to think of it: hey Zack, how many hours have you been on that stupid thing?"

Zombie Zack shuffled up from the basement and headed straight to the refrigerator. He grabbed a gallon of milk, some black forest ham, mustard and bread.

"At this time of night, kiddo?" Jason grinned. "Really?"

"Want some?" Zack looked up.

"Sure,"

Denise's phone buzzed. It was a text from Sandra: "Can we make next book club mtg Nov 12; just realized I can't do the 10th. Sorry!"

"No prob" Denise texted back. "Just make sure you wear fire-proof clothes for the *flaming* your book will get from She Who Must Not Be Named-- the world's biggest know it all crazy lady"

The phone buzzed again. It was Heather. "I'm in for the 12th!"

Again. "12th is fine" from Lauren.

Again. "I'm in" from Lynette.

Denise froze. Why were *other* Book Club members responding to this message?

"Shit shit shit shit shit!" she muttered.

Another: "Fine by me!" from Cathy.

Buzz: "Works for me" from Jackie.

Buzz. Personal text from Lauren: "Um, you do realize that was a group text, right?"

No kidding, Lauren. "I do now." Denise wrote back.

"Mom, where are the pickles?" asked Zack from the kitchen.

"Go to bed this minute or you are grounded!" Denise screamed. Zack took his sandwich and slinked up the stairs, making a face at Denise which, mercifully for Zack, she did not see. Denise's face was flushed with embarrassment. What the heck was she thinking when she wrote that stupid message? She really didn't even dislike Jackie that much; she was just fun to make fun of. Oh, golly, there was no good way out of this. Suck it up, sweetheart and do a little damage control. Her thumbs flew over her phone.

"Hey, gals, clearly I had a bit too much wine over here after book club! Please excuse my remarks. Looking forward to more lively discussions next month!" she sent out to the group.

A few girls wrote back chirpy notes about how fun it was to talk about the books. Lynette wrote something about how she felt bad that she had over-served everyone. Jackie wrote nothing more.

"Look, you don't even like this woman." Jason said after Denise explained the whole mess to him later. "So what's the big deal?"

"I was insulting; I was rude. I'm NOT a rude person." Denise wailed. She heard Zack burst into muffled laughter in the hallway upstairs. "Ok, funnyman: you're grounded." She called to him.

"C'mon, Denise, you've got to admit it's pretty funny." Jason said.

It was true. Denise knew she would have laughed herself silly had this happened to someone else. But it was her, and therefore it was of tragic proportions, or at least, a minor emergency.

Her phone buzzed. It was Jackie.

"Oh God, what am I going to do?" Denise needed more wine.

The message read: "Just out of curiosity, was that a Harry Potter reference in your text about me? I always thought of myself more as a McGonagall than a Voldemort."

Denise wrote, "At least you're not an asshole."

"Wanna bet?"

"I love Harry Potter. All three of my kids read the entire series."

"We should do *Sorcerer's Stone* in book club" replied Jackie.

"That's a fantastic idea!" wrote Denise, embellishing her message with heart emojis. A tad too precious than the exchange merited? Yes, but also necessary.

Denise turned all the lights off downstairs and went up to bed. Her head was going to be pounding tomorrow from all that wine. But Denise was a Mother of the Year, after all; she could handle it.

2. That Woman Is Me

The Whistler Park District Center, the $20 million pride of the eastern suburbs, nestled tastefully in among the oak trees of the forest preserve. With its flat horizontal lines and discreet windows, its design appeased even the perennially fussy Whistler Historical Society as well as the Zoning Committee, who had insisted that the new building "match the character of our unique village." The result was a faux cherry façade that appeared, at first blush, more like the entrance to a sprawling, but elegant lodge.

Interlocking paving stones (provided, at great expense after innumerable Village Board meetings) graced the parking lot and winding path to the Center's entrance. The gaps between these paving stones contained fine gravel that served as a filtration system for rainwater and melting snow. Any pollutants would be broken down in the gravel before the clean water run-off reached Otis Pond nearby. The result was that of an upscale architectural and environmental triumph that merely masqueraded as a practical building.

The building spanned an impressive 38,000 square feet. The main floor housed a state of the art Fitness Center, complete with treadmills and elliptical machines fitted with their own television monitors as well as USB outlets for smart phones. There was also a more traditional weight room for purists. Both the Men's and Women's Locker rooms contained discreet "family" areas for children to undress apart from the adults. There was also "Tot-time," the child-care facility for exercising parents. For a small fee, you could drop off your child, aged three months to twelve years, for an hour or two, while you ran or lifted weights or kick-boxed.

As one entered the facility, the Fitness Center and Track entrance were on the right, with the front desk, lounge area and locker room entrances on the left.

Cherry Tree Preschool took over much of the upper level, thought there was also a committed space for "active adult" programming ("classes include bridge, watercolors and tai chi, check our seasonal bulletin!"). Several of the function rooms upstairs could be rented out for birthday parties or other private events.

On the lower level, was a cavernous, multi-use hardwood gymnasium that could be curtained off into three separate full courts or six half-courts. Also on this level were two long mirrored rooms that served as a Group Fitness space (Zumba, yoga, kickboxing) in the mornings, doubling as youth dance instruction rooms (pre-ballet through "hippity-hop") in the afternoons.

Encircling the gymnasium from above was a one-eighth mile track. The Park District's website described it as having a "flash-track rolled rubber surface for running and walking." Windows around the track provided a view of Otis Pond, the paved parking lot, and the weight room, as one ran clockwise.

There was no swimming pool, the existence of which had been a multi-million dollar raspberry seed in the wisdom teeth of the Planning Committee as well as a sizeable group of concerned taxpayers. One particularly vocal Whistler resident, Janice Locke, delivered an impassioned speech to a village Trustees' meeting prior to initial ground-breaking, pointing out that neighboring towns possessed aquatic centers which brought in enormous revenue. Babies learned to love the water, teens learned valuable life-saving strategies, and seniors would have the opportunity to partake in water aerobics, which was, as everyone knew, far better for aging joints.

Janice was thanked for her dedication to Whistler's general wellness, but then regretfully reminded that low impact buoyancy came at a stiff price. Indeed, the addition of an aquatic center, at $4.5 million, would substantially increase the already sizeable burden upon the taxpayers of Whistler.

Trustee Monica Barnard had responded that aquatic centers were, putting it mildly, horrendous to deal with; not only was there the constant upkeep of maintaining and cleaning the water, and adjusting the chlorine levels, but there was also the issue of needing to hire a staff of trained lifeguards. Whistler resident Don Falco was then recognized. He was a retired engineer, who agreed: indoor pools were without a doubt the most expensive recreational spaces to construct.

"They need a special environment all to themselves. The money you'd need for moisture resistance in the walls alone would put costs through the roof."

Money was a ticklish point. Though Whistler was a fairly affluent suburb ("ideally located on the commuter train line to the city" according to the Whistler Chamber of Commerce's website), not all citizens were in favor of another tax referendum. Property taxes in Whistler were notoriously high.

"The Country Club has a pool, and so does the high school." Don continued. "Hell, my friend Teri has a pool." There was some good-natured chuckling throughout the room.

Money spent on an aquatic center was money that could not be used for environmentally beneficial pavers and faux cherry wood finish for the facade. Monica Barnard stated flatly: the proposed facility could either be aesthetically striking, in conformity with the stately beauty of Whistler and surrounding neighborhoods -- or it could have a pool. Ultimately, the Park District Planning Commission submitted their designs without an aquatic center. Even so, the referendum only narrowly passed, with 53.6% of voters in favor.

Joyce Carmody glided her silver BMW into the Park District parking lot, and pulled in between two minivans. Terry Gross' smooth voice, currently re-airing an old interview with David Sedaris, was silenced as Joyce turned off the ignition. She pushed the "lock" button on her key fob over her shoulder as she strode towards the Park District Center's entryway.

Joyce joked to her husband, Hal, that she hated running more than anything in life. Except being fat. And so she ran. Joyce wore navy running shorts and a grey tee shirt emblazoned with the mascot of the big university downstate. Joyce hated running, but she hated her thighs more. Joyce Ann Carmody (*nee* Sitek) may be getting older, my friends, but she was not getting any fatter. No more middle-aged spread for her, thank you very much. Joyce was 55, but could pass for forty on a good day, if she hadn't been drinking the night before, at least. That tended to make her eyes disappear under pillows of flesh.

She had started out by jogging down the sidewalks of Whistler, but Joyce had lived in the same house for almost twenty-five years. She couldn't stand it when her neighbors honked their horns at her when they passed, or texted her: "Hey, was that you jogging down Parkside Street today?" Thank God they finally had that new Park District building up, where Joyce's exercise habits were viewed only by others similarly engaged on the same track.

Every Monday, Wednesday and Friday, Joyce drove her 335i off Summit Road and onto winding path that marked the entry to the Park District facility. She had not partaken in the battle over its construction, though many of her neighbors had battled strenuously on either side. Joyce was not political, at least not in Whistler village politics. She loved this sweet little town, but Whistler's local intrigue drove her crazy, even after two decades' residency.

"Good morning," said a sallow young man with unusual hair, who sat at the front desk. He swiped Joyce's membership card and handed her a blinding white, but scratchy, towel. Joyce wrapped her car keys in the towel; she would later place it on a windowsill midway around the track. Today was a counter-clockwise day according to the arrow. She stepped onto the track: alrighty then.

It was nine-fifteen, which meant that Joyce would overhear the end of morning Bootcamp in the gym below, but would be gone before the men started playing their lunchtime basketball games. There was the usual sprinkling of middle-aged to elderly walkers on the track. Most of the hardcore "real runner" types, those wiry-muscled demi-gods, had already completed their daily half-marathons or whatever they ran. The building opened at five in the morning especially for these strange people.

One of the few things Joyce disliked more than running was early morning wake-ups. Her boys were out of the house now; she could theoretically sleep till noon. Hal was not a morning person either, but he liked maintaining a regular schedule, which, for him, included juice and eggs on weekday mornings before catching the train at the Idlewood Lane stop nearby. Joyce, who only merely tolerated eggs rather than enjoying them, joined Hal when he scrambled them but passed when he prepared them over-easy. On running mornings, like today, Joyce tried not to eat anything.

Before meeting Chris and having the boys, Joyce had begun a career as an academic. Specifically, she had started worked towards a Ph.D. in History, specializing in Gender and Power in the Lives of early 16th Century Spanish Nuns. While Joyce Sitek conducted research on early modern women and monasticism, she lectured in massive Western Civilization surveys at the university downstate, as well as teaching some History of Women courses at satellite schools sprinkled amid some of the area's community colleges. While tailgating with some law students, Ph.D. candidate Joyce met the university's favorite son, Hal Carmody, and the rest, pardon the expression, was history. Joyce never taught another Western Civilization Survey course again.

Hal was coasting through law school with a gentlemen's Cs that belied his true intelligence. He was instantly smitten by raucous, curvy Joyce and her rapid-fire banter. She, in turn, was taken with Hal's good-natured rapport and latent ambition. Hal was a fourth generation Carmody, of the real estate magnate Carmodys and the university's Carmody Dining Hall that squatted in granite splendor on the school's North Quad. By the time springtime rolled through campus, the two were engaged, and just after Christmas, they were married.

With Hal's obviously pedigreed muscle, Joyce could now teach any course she desired; she could probably be named Chair of the History Department, but the newlyweds decided that any position by Joyce would smack of nepotism. We don't want to give the Trustees the appearance of any impropriety, said Hal. Joyce was frankly grateful; she loved to lecture about paradigm shifts in Early Modern Europe, but had no stomach for the onslaught of administrative roles that faculty members needed to fill. She lacked the passion and ambition required for full-time academia, she admitted.

"I don't want to be on the Honors Committee, or the Search Committee, or the Faculty Outreach Committee. I don't want to have to go to conferences four times a year and chase publications." She said to Hal as they planned their honeymoon in Barcelona and Madrid. "Let's just do our own thing and have a family."

And raise a family they did. The couple settled down in a sprawling newly-constructed home in the eastern suburb of Whistler. Hal and Joyce produced, in rapid succession, two ridiculously large, good-natured boys named Will and Tyler, with wide hands, freckles, and large feet. The boys grew up loving, loveable, trouble-making and exasperating. Joyce's days and years were filled with soccer carpools, PTO fundraisers, Boy Scouts, and Saint Jerome's Youth Camps. For Will, there were Marching Band concerts (clarinet), and for Tyler, football boosters (defensive end). They grew. Will was taller and lankier, Ty broad-shouldered and thicker.

In high school, the Carmody boys excelled at soccer, video games, ribald humor, and under-age drinking. When the time came they went, of course, to college downstate, eating their meals in the Carmody Dining Hall financed by their great-grandfather. Will majored in Marketing and two years later, Tyler majored in Psychology. Both boys went Greek, though in different houses (Sig Ep and Phi Tau, respectively), both drifted on and off academic probation, but both, finally and to Joyce's utmost relief, graduated.

One of the partners at Hal's law firm arranged an interview for Tyler at Dean Witter, and soon he was a respectable young stock broker with an apartment in the City and an upwardly mobile career, if you could believe that. Will was busily working his way up at a company called Synergy Media, doing God knows what, but who cared: he was employed. Joyce was relieved and delighted with their success, or at least their lack of imminent failure. Although she privately believed that jobs that did not require advanced degrees were not worth attaining, Joyce could not visualize either Will or Tyler pursuing graduate school in any form. Thank God they had the Trust Fund in case one or both of them did something stupid. Not that she wanted to jinx them or anything, but Joyce knew her boys.

With this lap, it was four times around; only twenty more to go. The Park District posted signs at every corner, admonishing runners and walkers not to spit or use their cell phones. Evidently, the spitting prohibition was the only regulation the walkers and runners abided by. There were no visible signs of spittle, but cell phone use was rampant.

Joyce could hear the Bootcamp instructor downstairs encouraging his victims, "Ok, twenty more seconds, now fifteen, ten, five four three two one! Alright, now the other side!"

She passed by an elderly couple who held hands as they walked, and wore matching green track suits. The woman was tiny and hunched, while the man strode with almost military

21

posture. With a slight shock, Joyce noticed that the woman had lumps covering the back of her neck, almost like skin tags, but bigger. She barely came up to her companion's shoulder.

As she rounded a corner, Joyce passed a pair of elegant-looking women in their thirties, who were gesticulating as they walked. One wore a shimmering lavender hijab; the other had her hair pulled back in what the kids called a "messy bun." Each wore crimson lipstick.

"How do you prepare it? With butter?" asked one.

"What you've got to do, Gabi, is sear it skin-side down. That's the best way to get the full . . ." the voice faded as Joyce passed.

God, Joyce thought, she'd better not listen or she'd start getting hungry. Who talks about recipes when they're supposed to be exercising? Maybe that was their therapy. Those ladies looked to be in perfect shape, though, in their leggings and tank tops. Not a saddle-bag in sight. And they were probably born that way too, Joyce thought. Effortless beauty.

Ruefully, Joyce would have loved a cigarette. Nothing about running felt as good as a cigarette tasted on that first inhale, or that satisfying billow of exhalation. Of course, her decades-long habit of cigarettes was another reason why Joyce was at the track.

Joyce and Hal had gloriously smoked together for a few years, Hal playing a debonair Cary Grant, would always bow before lighting her Marlboro Light. Most men Joyce met hadn't liked cigarette smoking, preferring nasty, noxious cigars so popular during that abrasively masculine culture of steakhouses and mahogany that flourished in the 1990s.

Cigarettes had seen Joyce through the initial research and drafting of her dissertation (completed, though never formally defended when she abandoned academia), her Field Exams and her teaching load. Vats of black coffee ran a close second place. Hal, exhibiting again his endearing yet annoying characteristic of having everything come easily to him, quit painlessly in tandem with his father's diagnosis of heart disease.

Hal urged Joyce to quit with him, and she agreed -- until the next occasion arose when she wanted another cigarette. Out of respect for Hal's sacrifice, Joyce no longer smoked in their home, confining her cigarettes to the car or when she was out with friends. Joyce's feeling was that, if you didn't do something in the privacy of your own home, then it couldn't properly be deemed a bad habit; it was merely a behavior one indulged in every now and then. She never let the boys witness her smoking, and she kept air freshener in her purse and glove compartment to help mask it from them. Neither Ty nor Will ever mentioned it to Joyce, but then again, they always seemed to be in their own little world of rough-housing and smart talk.

Doubtless, her husband could smell the tobacco on her clothes and in her hair, but dear Hal said nothing. Instead, he placidly regaled Joyce with how much better he felt now, and how many points his blood pressure had dropped.

Two years after Hal quit smoking, his father died while undergoing quadruple bypass surgery. Grief over the loss of his "Pop" added to the poignancy of Hal's anti-smoking crusade. After Pop's funeral, Joyce cut down considerably, knowing her lighting up was perhaps the utmost in bad taste given the circumstances.

And then, around the time of her fiftieth birthday, Joyce quit smoking without any fanfare, thinking that any announcement she made might jinx her chance of success. Besides, she didn't "really" smoke; she just had occasional cigarettes, so she would really need to quit anything that wasn't actually a practice. And thus the thirty year love affair ended. Will had graduated from college and was now in an apartment in the city. His brother would soon be graduating as well, despite his seemingly best efforts to keep his grades on the dim side of acceptability.

Joyce knew it was inevitable that she would gain some weight as a result of stopping smoking; every woman who quit seemed to say so. Hal, of course, had not gained an ounce, but Hal was also the sort of person who could switch to only salads

23

at lunch for a week and lose three pounds. This was when Joyce first began to work out, dutifully purchasing a yoga mat and doing her "hundreds" at Pilates. That the timing of this profound lifestyle change coincided with Ty's college graduation was not lost on Joyce one iota. Former students of European History understand the merits of symbolism.

Her scruffy frat boy birds were now both officially out of the nest, not too far away of course, but they no longer put Whistler down as their home address. They visited often on weekends, meeting up with old friends from Whistler High School. Joyce dutifully cleaned their laundry, glad to be needed again and wondering how on earth her babies would make it as adults.

The trouble was, life felt hollow without Tyler or Will snoring deafeningly in the corner bedroom. Joyce felt as if she'd been walking on the suburban equivalent of an airport moving sidewalk for the past two decades or so, with the conveyer belt pulling her ever-forward. Now the end of the moving walkway was coming up fast and Joyce had to poise herself properly. Would she keep her pace once she transitioned to the linoleum, or go down sprawling?

Not long ago, as she sat with Hal and Will, searching for Tyler's grinning face amid row upon row of black-robed and mortar-boarded students filing in to Pomp and Circumstance, Joyce felt her first hot flash. It was a rising burn, as if she were suddenly mortified and furiously blushing, starting at the back of her head, at the hairline, and sweeping across her neck and cheeks. Sweat began to drizzle down her back. Joyce thought maybe it was just the heat of the day; she took off her light cardigan and fanned herself with a program. The burning diminished after a few minutes and, as she applauded her firstborn son's milestone passage, Joyce forgot about the incident.

At the party they threw for Ty later that afternoon, Joyce felt inexplicably warm once again. Maybe it was because she was drinking so much, both in relief that her younger boy had made it through school, and because she and Hal had invited a volatile combination of relatives on both sides. Joyce put her glass of chardonnay up to her burning cheek and smiled bleakly at Hal, as his brother Trevor flirted with Joyce's niece, who was probably thirty years his junior. Sweet Jesus, somebody needed to keep Trevor away from the booze, if only for today. Her boys were better behaved than this man, and God knew Will and Ty Carmody were no gentlemen.

Another hot flash woke Joyce up that night at two-thirty, and again at four. Then it started happening every night. As if by clockwork, full-on menopause had struck. The cessation of periods after about forty years was at least welcome, but the accompanying symptoms were terrifying. Joyce felt like she had awakened one morning in someone else's body. She sprouted a layer of fine hair over her entire face; the near-constant hot flashes left her damp and shivering; she gained thirty pounds in addition to her post-smoking weight gain. Her violent mood swings and crying jags left Hal baffled. Their sex life became a vague memory. Hormonal changes gave Joyce offensive-smelling perspiration. She started waking up five or six times a night.

Hal was awakened one night to see Joyce hunched over the side of the bed, her body heaving with sobs.

"What is it? Are you alright? What happened?" he asked.

"It's not the weather; they're hot flashes!" she wailed.

Hal was mystified. "Oh. You feel warm. Is that all?"

"Fuck off."

Trying to explain the complex loops of embarrassment and acceptance and her own feelings about her lack of desirability and lack of womanliness were too difficult to articulate. Joyce knew, as a feminist and a scholar, that a woman was not defined by her capacity to reproduce. She was not a creature based only on menstrual cycles. But then again, on a certain level, she sort of was. Menopause was too easy a target for humor, just like menstrual cycles and PMS. No wonder that lady's been so bitchy lately; she's all menopausal, ha-ha, isn't that hilarious? See that woman all sweaty and wearing a bathing suit in the dead of winter? Ha-ha, another hot flash! See, it's silly! Aren't old ladies funny? Joyce watched television and wept in recognition: "I'm an Un-woman!" she cried during *The Handmaids Tale*.

Joyce thought: you go from being sweet to being smart to being sexy to being maternal. And then you end up being comical before you enter that final phase of your life when you'll be infantilized as the sweet little old lady. Doubtless wearing a cute floppy old lady hat and addressing everyone as "sweetie." So this was it; she'd passed through being maternal. It wasn't as if Joyce even wanted any more children, and her boys were (hopefully) nowhere near being ready to be parents. So there she was, in the looming No Man's Land (har har) between Maternity and Senility.

Worse still, Joyce had no desire whatsoever to be a wife in any sense of the term, other than the basics of sharing a home and a master bathroom. Even her girlfriends, who used to make her happy with their banter and laughter, now annoyed her. Joyce begged off on any invitations to lunches or girls' nights out.

In a frantic attempt to do something that made her feel good, Joyce had baked loaves of fresh sourdough bread, ate them with melting butter, then sat weeping on the sofa, licking her buttery fingers. It wasn't just that she had lost her status as a reproductive female, that her babies were "grown and flown" and now living and working (good lord how on earth did they manage it?) in the city; it was that she couldn't seem to move. Depression enveloped Joyce like a heavy blanket. She was a mother without children; a wife who couldn't stand her husband to even touch her. Always a curvy woman, Joyce had previously dwelt on the rounder side of average. Now she had a pot belly like the old women in the park. She sat on the sofa, surfed the internet and cried as all her pairs of jeans became too tight.

Talking to her mother only irritated Joyce. Roberta Sitek had no recollection of any downside to her fifties whatsoever, and remembered menopause as "one of the best times" of her life. "Oh, I didn't really get any hot flashes, hon. Are you sure that's what you're having? Maybe you just drink too much wine. That can do it too, you know."

Joyce spent hours scouring the web for some good news, any good news. But in 2017, good news was difficult for a feminist to find; frankly, good news was hard to find for most sentient beings in 2017. Joyce blamed her further weight gain squarely on the Presidential Election of 2016. To which dear Hal would always infuriatingly reply: "I know, he's awful, but you gotta admit that at least the market kind of loves him."

Joyce sampled bee pollen and essential oils and vitamin supplements, joined chat groups on Facebook (mercifully set to "private" so her friends and family wouldn't see that Joyce was a member of "Women over Fifty" and "Menopause Support Group International"). The groups were vaguely charming. For example, Joyce learned that, in the UK, women called their affliction hot "flushes" instead of flashes. Eventually, the women in the support groups irritated Joyce as well. Everything irritated her. Hal's bad habits, tolerable for twenty-five years, became unbearably magnified. Good lord, the snoring! For the love of God, no more hard boiled eggs! Those socks on the floor, seriously?

"Honey, you look so pretty tonight," Hal would say, trying to put his arms around her.

"Are you kidding me?" and Joyce would roll over.

Eighteen laps. She was over two miles now. Running was one of the few times that Joyce did not feel self-conscious about being over-heated. She sweated so much when she worked out that it hardly mattered if she had a hot flash there on the track.

The tall man and his lumpy wife finished their walk and left the track. Joyce puffed past an ancient bald-headed man, swinging his arms wildly as he strode, his pink scalp peppered with liver spots.

"Looks like you're getting pretty warm there, young lady," he quipped.

How was she supposed to respond to that, Joyce wondered. What was she expected to do, laugh? Yes, indeed, sir, I am at a track and I am working out. So sorry. Or maybe she was just being psycho again; maybe the man was lonely and merely making conversation. It didn't matter; he was behind her now.

A trio of young-ish looking women walking abreast partially blocked the "Run" aisle. Their clothes were so similar (black workout leggings with sheer panel cut-outs, paired with tunic-style tank tops) that Joyce wondered if they had texted each other prior to visiting the Park District. From the bits of conversation Joyce overheard as she jogged by, these women were ready for blood.

"It's a disgrace that they put Matthew into Advanced Math, instead of Accelerated Math." One said.

"How is he ever going to be properly challenged?" said the next.

"You have to petition for a change." The third added. "If he's not tracked for Accelerated Math now, by the time he gets into middle school it'll be too--"

Their voices faded behind Joyce, who really wanted to keep listening to this one. Oh, ladies, it you think you've got challenges now, wait till little Matthew starts smoking weed behind your neighbor's rhododendron bushes. But sure, you just keep complaining about your little guy not being sufficiently challenged.

Will and Tyler were never trouble-makers, though. They had simply been boisterous boys with a privileged background and too much free time growing up. At least they had mostly missed the whole cellphone addiction until they were well into their teens. These days you could see literal babies with their own phones.

Her boys should have had a place like *this* growing up, Joyce thought. They'd been stuck with that ramshackle old

YMCA in town for all their activities growing up here in town. If those stupid Whistler trustees hadn't been battling the stupid zoning people, and if the original Referendum to subsidize the Park District building had passed the first time, then Ty and Will might at least have gotten some use out of the facility in high school.

Bootcamp finished up on the lower level and Joyce glanced down as the exhausted campers high-fived each other. "Thank you all for your energy," the instructor said into her microphone. "Can you feel how much you're growing and have already grown? Your strength inspires me! Each day you go a little farther, and it's beautiful to watch. See you next time. Make sure you have plenty of lean protein and hydrate yourselves properly."

As the Bootcamp class put away their mats and free weights and kettle balls, a preschool class was being led into the other end of the gymnasium. The children played freeze tag to songs, appropriately enough, from *Frozen*.

Hal had gotten Joyce her membership at the Park District Center last year, after a mortifying, wine-enhanced heart-to-heart one Saturday night started to turn things around for her at last. Hal prevailed upon Joyce to seek medical help for her menopause and her depression and her mood swings and her hot flashes and anything else that might give him back the sassy gal he married. Joyce picked herself up from where the moving sidewalk had deposited her, and went to see a doctor.

"Ok, Mrs. Carmody, can you tell me how you've been feeling lately?" the nurse had asked. Joyce shocked both of them by bursting into immediate tears.

"I don't know who I am anymore!" she wailed. "I don't know anything anymore; help me!"

Hormones and antidepressants and counselling combined to help transform Joyce back into a human being again. She bought a Fitbit and monitored her steps religiously. Joyce started out by walking the indoor track at the Park District Center, but after a few months, she wanted to reach her daily

29

step goals faster, so she upped the ante by running. Nothing fast, of course, but it was running. Her lungs burned in protest, but she kept at it and started losing a little of that extra weight. Joyce began to feel, if not good, certainly better than she had in quite a while.

"You know, plenty of women consider this a sign of prestige," Hal offered.

"What? Losing their minds?" Joyce had asked.

"No, you goofball: seeking medical help. Think of how lucky you are to have access to this kind of stuff."

Hal always had a sensible answer to problems. She *was* lucky to have all the meds. Not to mention the massages and pedicures that Joyce indulged in; though not entirely necessary, they helped put the pieces back together. Over all, Joyce had the sneaking suspicion that she had somehow dodged a potentially ruinous bullet. She was almost giddy with relief.

A few years back, when the boys were still in high school, Will had failed his driver's test not once, but twice. The poor guy froze up when he had to parallel park; no matter how many times Will flawlessly maneuvered their car in the driveway and street, when he got to the DMV he got a mental block and blew it. The state only allowed three attempts at passing the driving exam; if he failed again, the state would instead extend his Learner's Permit, thereby potentially ruining Will's social status forever. He was mortified and frozen with the possibility that this last attempt could be his undoing. He hadn't even wanted to try again because of the possibility of failing, but Hal had been his usual patient, calming self and convinced their firstborn not to give up. Despite Will's throwing up before the test, he passed it without any great fanfare and became a bona fide legal driver.

Tyler, in predictable mocking style, held an imaginary microphone under Will's chin. "William Christopher Carmody, you just dodged one helluva bullet. What will you do now?" he asked in a newscaster's voice.

"Dude, I'm going to Disneyland." Will replied, like the old commercial. Joyce had swatted at Ty's behind, but she laughed almost shrilly with relief. It was the same sort of lightness she felt now, after going to a doctor and admitting she had reached a treacherous roadblock.

Twenty-four laps was three miles. Ha! She still had not reached a point at which the completion of a run did not astound and delight her. Three miles! At her age! Joyce grabbed a towel as she walked a cool-down lap, and wiped her streaming face. Her grey tee had a dark yoke of sweat staining it, but so did that guy speed-walking over there. And that young girl over on the stationary bike, with an emaciated body and sheer purple Lululemon tights, was red-faced and panting. All of them here at the Park District were all in the same boat, after all, weren't they? Ok, maybe Joyce wouldn't count the three uptight biddies with the accelerated math discussion, but they hardly mattered.

Now that Joyce was no longer continually buffeted and at the mercy of her changing body, she felt ready to face any new challenge. She paused at the cork bulletin board on the east wall of the entryway before getting back to her car. Amid the photos of lost pets and requests for babysitters, there was an announcement for a charity three-on-three basketball tournament to be played at the Park District Building coming up soon. "Take to the Courts for a Great Cause!" the posters read. "No matter what your age or skill-set, we will place you in a fair and competitive division."

Joyce was inspired: maybe Hal and a couple of his buddies could enter the tournament? Joyce would gather Shannon and a couple of her other girlfriends and they'd cheer for their middle-aged husbands on the courts. It sounded like a hoot. She walked back to her car, mentally figuring out Hal's team for him; only those buddies whose wives she liked, of course.

Joyce's phone buzzed. It was a text message from Tyler, an unusual occurrence, especially in the morning. Please God, let him not be in any trouble, Joyce prayed silently. Ty was such a free spirit. He was born with a little extra shot of adrenaline or something. Both Joyce and Hal thought that city living and embarking in his new career, with all the responsibilities that entailed, had calmed their younger boy down a bit. He couldn't have crashed his car; he took public transportation to work. It was too early in the year for him to be asking for Christmas present ideas; the boys usually waited until December 22nd or so for that.

"Hey, Mama --" the text read. "Quick question: where do you think I could get a nice diamond ring?"

Instead of texting Tyler back, which, Ty had told her, all people under forty preferred, Joyce called her son back before unlocking the BMW.

"Please tell me you're asking me this because you want to get me a birthday present." She said when he picked up.

Ty laughed. "Not this time, Mom," he cried. "I'm going to ask Katie to marry me."

Despite the cool of the morning air, Joyce felt a hot flash begin to creep up the back of her neck. She sank behind the wheel, wishing she'd brought an extra towel from home. And a carton of cigarettes. And a bottle of vodka. Each day, she thought, each day we go a little farther.

3. Be Happy Still

The woman wore a bright red fleece jacket, zipped all the way up to her chin, and a pair of grey sweatpants. On her head was a baseball cap, and in her hand was a leash. She had just finished walking her elderly Golden Retriever through the park. He'd met a doggie friend and run around a bit off-leash. Good for him, the woman thought. Poor pup's getting old; he needs all the playtime he can get. There was a muffled tone and the woman fumbled in her jacket pockets.

"Oh, hey there, honey," Karen spoke into her cellphone. "I'm out with the dog right now, but I'll be getting back home in about a half an hour. Well, he was asleep when I left, but I know he'll wake up to see you and his little buddy. See you around lunch time, then? Uh-huh. Yes, they'll be coming by. I'll call them back later. Oh, of course, he's too little to understand all this right now. Oh, yes, much easier. See you soon, hon."

Karen sighed deeply and slipped her cellphone back into her jacket pocket. The dog, Goose, looked at her with his honey-colored eyes, cocking his head questioningly.

"It's Ok, love, don't worry." Karen said to him.

The wind was picking up. She'd better get going. The two proceeded up the Bowl and out of Bartleby Park. Goose knew the route, and started padding down Larch Place and back home, but Karen noticed a familiar stooped figure bagging leaves around the corner on Chester and pulled Goose around. They started towards the figure, who picked her rake back up and set to work on the far side of the lawn.

"Howdy, Stranger," Karen called out to Ann-Marie, who hadn't looked up from her raking when Karen approached. When she saw Karen and Goose, Ann-Marie dropped her rake and stretched her back side to side before greeting them at the sidewalk.

"Well, look at you, out and about! Your knee must be doing better." Ann-Marie noted.

"Well, I got this special cream that I put on every night and it's been doing the trick. Not nearly as stiff in the mornings as it's been." Karen replied. "I got it online; it's from China. Supposedly, it's a miracle cure out there."

"Isn't that something?"

"Hey, where are your manners, Goose?" Karen admonished her mild-faced companion as he lifted a leg onto Ann-Marie's impatiens.

"Aw, Goose is a good boy, aren't you?" Ann-Marie asked rhetorically, scratching the dog beneath his chin as Goose closed his eyes rapturously. "I don't mind about those flowers."

Karen and Ann-Marie had known each other for years, without ever becoming real friends. They'd exchanged pleasantries, and knew many details about the particularities of each other's life in the way of polite conversation, but it was a limited relationship, mostly tallied by waves and brief greetings. Nevertheless, each fully enjoyed their short chats, centering largely on family, health, and weather.

"So how've things been going, aside from keeping your lawn the neatest in town?" Karen asked.

"Oh, these leaves," Ann-Marie groaned. "I'm out here every day; the minute I get it cleared, that stupid tree drops more, so I have to come out here and do it all over again. It's enough to drive you to drink."

"That's why I don't bother," Karen replied, pretending she didn't notice the disapproving glance Ann-Marie shot her. "I have the boys from Emperor Landscaping come in once a week in the fall. They come out with a crew of three young fellas, and in twenty minutes it's all done, including the driveway. Unbelievable."

"Aren't they expensive?" Ann-Marie asked.

Karen chuckled. "Don talked them into a senior discount last year. I told him that maybe *he* needed it, but I was far too young to qualify. But, a discount's a discount; who am I to argue?"

Karen and Don Falco were perhaps the cheapest residents of Whistler. Until fairly recently, when Don's health started to deteriorate, he had been a local celebrity of sorts, constantly voicing opposition to the spate of expensive projects Whistler's Village Trustees seemed always to come up with. It must have irked him when that Park District referendum went through. Their taxes in this town were crazy, but you had to admit, the finished products looked pretty good.

"So, have you heard from Beth lately? That baby of hers has got to be, what, two now?" Ann-Marie asked.

"Oh, my goodness, yes! Liam turned two last August; lemme show you some pictures Beth just sent to me." Karen fumbled with her cellphone for a few seconds, then displayed some photos of a beaming toddler. "Look at those cheeks, will you? Beth and Rick are just the luckiest parents ever; their little guy is so smart. Liam does that sign language thing, have you heard about this? They teach babies sign language. So Liam can tell them when he wants to eat or when he wants more by giving them hand signals!"

"Can't he talk?" Ann-Marie was confused.

"Of course he can talk, but Beth was explaining it to me: for children's cognitive development, it's easier for them to do the sign language than use their words sometimes. So she

35

teaches him sign language. *Everybody* does it now" Karen frowned and looked exasperated.

"I guess I don't understand all that," Ann-Marie replied. "Pete's kids are growing up so far away."

"Well, you will soon enough." her frost melted. "Just you wait; your daughter's going to have all sorts of babies and you'll get to spoil them all rotten, just like I do. Oh, my goodness, it's the most fun I've had in years. But wow, do these new parents over-think everything. It's a whole new world out there for babies than when we were young mamas. I told Beth how she used to crawl around on the floor of the backseat of our old Pontiac, and she nearly fainted. These days, we'd get arrested for that." The two women laughed together.

"Hey, didn't you tell me the other day that you were going to help out with the auditions for the play last night?" Ann-Marie asked. For a number of years now, Karen had worked on the board of the local community theater group. They mounted four productions a year, mostly crowd-pleasers by Neil Simon or an occasional whodunit for fun. Being a community theater group dependent upon volunteers for their successes or failures, the Little Theater's productions varied, sometimes wildly, in quality. In Karen's opinion, which she was not shy about sharing, their successes largely correlated to her being cast in, or allowed to direct, a given production. She was even occasionally correct in this assessment.

"I did! And were we ever surprised by the turn out." Karen barely paused for breath. "I think Whistler Little Theater should have considered doing *Steel Magnolias* years ago, so many women came out. All the age ranges too; I was worried we might get too many old ones and not enough young."

"That's a wonderful movie." said Ann-Marie. "I loved Shirley MacLaine in it. That's going to be a good one for you folks. Don't forget to let me know when the performances are; I'll want to see that one."

"You know, if you volunteer to help out with concessions or selling tickets, you can get in free. I'm in charge of the Hospitality Committee and we're always looking for help. I think you'd really enjoy it."

"You know, that's a good idea." Ann-Marie responded, then she looked serious. "Tell, me Karen, how is Don doing?"

Karen's smile faded somewhat in the corners. "Well, I'll be honest with you, Ann-Marie: it's rough. He has some good days and he has some days when he's lucky I don't murder him." Karen laughed again. "But he was able to sit outside and enjoy the sunshine last weekend before it started getting too cold. I know he'd like to be out with Goose, running around the park with a ball, but he can't even keep up with this old pooch."

"He's lucky he's got you around."

"Ha. Tell that to him. From Don's point of view, I'm digging him an early grave with my cooking. I told him to go pound sand." Karen laughed again.

"Well, I'd better get this done if I want to have any time left to do my other work today," said Ann-Marie, walking back to her rake.

"Good chatting with you, Ann-Marie." Called Karen, tugging at Goose's leash. The dog had spread himself out on the grass with his muzzle resting on his forepaws. Goose turned a reproachful glance at Karen, then rose to his feet, shaking his head till his tags jingled.

"You too. Give my best to Don."

Woman and dog rounded the corner at Larch and then disappeared from view. Poor Karen. Her husband was not well. His pancreas; you rarely heard any happy endings with pancreas stories. It was usually a year or less, which Karen surely knew. That was probably why she spent so much of her free time volunteering with that theater group lately. The time that Karen spent worrying about costumes and ticket sales and program editing was time that she didn't spend thinking about having to say goodbye to her man far too soon.

It really wasn't fair; these were the years they were supposed to be enjoying together. Finally, their kids were all grown up with families of their own. Of course everybody in town knew about the time Don had gotten in trouble with the government for his taxes years ago, but Ann-Marie was certain that was all fine now. Their girl, Beth, was a teacher for Special Needs children; you didn't get more giving than that. And now Beth was married and had that cute little boy with the chubby cheeks. Poor Donny, instead of taking his grandkid to baseball games and playing golf in Florida like every other retiree, he was probably getting some awful chemotherapy cocktail every week and feeling terrible. Those so-called treatments ended up hurting people more than the actual disease; sometimes Ann-Marie wondered how doctors could get away with that.

You just never knew, that was the bottom line, Ann-Marie thought. Just a few minutes before talking to Karen, she had seen Mrs. Whiteside go by. That was another sad story. If you looked deep enough, Ann-Marie figured, everybody had a sad story somewhere. She'd had her own tough break, losing Bo when he was barely even seventy. That a heart attack had felled Bo Frain was not a shock to anyone, given his size and affection for beer, French fries and chili, but no one expected it to come quite so soon. And yet there are some people out there, smoking cigarettes and eating junk food and living to be a hundred. It just makes you mad.

Ann-Marie filled two large Menards leaf bags and dragged them to the edge of the driveway, where three other bags already stood. Garbage pick-up was tomorrow morning. Now that Ann-Marie had stopped bending and filling, she felt chilled by the cool breeze. She put the rake in the shed and went back inside the house. It was getting near the time of her call with Kelly.

Coffee would be nice, but Ann-Marie didn't want to jinx anything at the moment. Until she got the results back from her doctor, she was laying off the coffee for a bit. Jeanette McElroy had given Ann-Marie a scare recently at her annual exam, noting her dense breast tissue.

"Hmm," she had said, pressing her cold fingers gently on Ann-Marie's chest beneath the paper robe.

"Hmm?"

"Do you drink a lot of coffee," Dr. McElroy had asked.

"Maybe four of five cups a day," Ann-Marie admitted. Dr. McElroy had whooped in response. She was younger than Ann-Marie, maybe still in her forties, though it was hard to tell these days, since nobody ever seemed to look their age. Jeanette had auburn-tinted hair and an athletic build and always wore shoes with funny designs on them; the last time Ann-Marie saw Dr. McElroy, she'd worn leopard print flats. Ann-Marie guessed it was boring wearing scrubs, so Jeanette jazzed things up with her footwear.

"Good lord, no wonder you've got all this going on. At your age, your breast tissue shouldn't be so firm. Let's schedule you for a mammogram and figure this out." She'd said briskly. "In the meantime, cut back on the coffee, for the love of Pete!"

The mammogram, however, had come back with some questionable dark shadows, so Jeannette had ordered a routine biopsy, which had been terribly painful. Ann-Marie had laid in bed with cooling pads on her chest, like a young woman with mastitis or something. They were waiting on the labs from that right now.

Ann-Marie knew that, at her age (she admitted to being sixty-three), she became more and more likely to get some form of cancer every year she lived. Especially breast cancer. It seemed Ann-Marie knew over a dozen friends, and probably twenty acquaintances who'd had to endure it over the years. Most got through it battered and grim, but ultimately triumphant. A few were less fortunate. It was remarkable, though, the treatments they had these days. They detected problems earlier, and did all that reconstructive surgery. Women weren't ashamed to mention mastectomies anymore, not like when Ann-Marie had grown up. Of course, Ann-Marie didn't want a bad diagnosis; nobody did.

Ann-Marie had a very important reason to want to stay well. She had to be healthy for the baby, Kelly and Andy's baby. What good is a grandmother if she can't run the ship when the new mom comes home from the hospital, sleep-deprived and overwhelmed with responsibilities and hormones? She would go to the new parents, armed with baby wipes and extra diapers and boring stories of raising her Kelly and Sean, and boss them around like a grandma should. Ann-Marie couldn't wait.

The rust-colored armchair by the window creaked slightly when Ann-Marie eased herself down with a cup of Celestial Seasonings herbal tea (Raspberry Zing). She and Kelly talked almost every morning, usually after Kelly finished up her "Sunrise Yoga" class, which started at the ungodly hour of six a.m. Ann-Marie never really saw the point of yoga; if you were going to be up so early, you may as well *do* something. Lying on your back and breathing deeply like they did in those yoga studios was pretty much just paying someone to sleep. Of course, living in a condo in the city, like Kelly and Andy did, it's not like they could water any flowerbeds from up there on the twenty-third floor, or prune any hedges. In true Kelly fashion, of course, she'd turned family planning into something to get upset about.

"Shouldn't that be the easy part?" Ann-Marie had said laughingly to her daughter. "I thought people were supposed to enjoy it."

She should have known better than to joke with Kelly when she had a bee in her bonnet. Ann-Marie had to listen and exclaim as Kelly went on about cycles and secretions and timing until Ann-Marie had felt like she was watching an episode of ER.

Kelly had always been a bag of nerves, though, ever since she was tiny. She worried about the squirrels staying warm enough in the winter; she worried about saving endangered manatees; she worried about her little friends not liking her enough. And then in high school, she had gotten actual panic attacks before final exams. She'd retaken her SATs twice just to get borderline decent scores. That was in the old days, before every teenager got special medication for what they used to call a normal life experience. Poor Kelly. Remember how she was so crazy before her wedding? Brides are generally uptight, but Kelly had been a shaking, pallid nervous wreck. No wonder the poor thing needed yoga to relax.

Kelly's baby would not be Ann-Marie's first grandchild; her son Sean already had little Josh and Caroline, but they were all the way across the country in California. Ann-Marie wanted her first *local* grandchild, only twenty minutes away in the city. It was no secret that she got along better with Kelly anyway. Sean always had to do his own thing, never listening to any advice from Ann-Marie and Bo, before Bo died two years ago (during his afternoon nap on the sofa, what a nice way to go, Ann-Marie thought).

Sean had not been nervous one bit about his wedding, though God knows, he should have been. He married that Rebecca woman, who anyone could see was crazy and manipulative and would ruin his life. But why bother listening to your parents when you can make a terrible mistake all on your own? Boys are just different from girls, though. They don't take things to heart the same way. Maybe if Ann-Marie and Bo had told Sean that they loved Rebecca, he'd have dropped her. Instead, they'd sat Sean down and explained to him that Rebecca was trash, so naturally, he married her immediately. To add insult to injury, then, they moved to California.

Worse still, Rebecca was overweight, not in a cute plump way, but in a slovenly, slightly greasy way. Ann-Marie felt a little bad for thinking this way about family, but the fact of the matter was: Rebecca was a slob. She dressed like a fat girl, wearing an array of flowy, jersey cloth shirts that molded around her massive breasts and billowed to mid-thigh. She paired these tops with implausibly dainty, lace-bottomed leggings that appeared to scream in protest of her thighs. When Rebecca was pregnant, Sean had sent monthly photographs to Ann-Marie, documenting the shocking growth of Rebecca's pale belly, adorned with cute little signs reading "two months" and "seven months."

41

Thank God, Josh and Caroline, her faraway grandchildren, turned out alright. At nine and seven, both appeared to be normal kids, only vaguely resembling Rebecca, with her wide mouth and ginger hair. Both were little blondies like Sean had been as a youngster. Ann-Marie had been out to visit Sean and the kids a few times over the years, taking them to Disneyland and Sea World and Lego-land. The kids had been frenetic and over-stimulated, but what do you expect at Disneyland when you're six?

During Ann-Marie's (weekly, at best) calls with Sean, he told her that little Caroline whined and was a picky eater, which was hilarious considering that Rebecca had clearly never met a meal she didn't like. Sean flatly stated that if the kids wouldn't eat what Rebecca put out for them, then they wouldn't eat. To Ann-Marie, it seemed a sign that Caroline had good taste to turn her nose up at the cheese-covered, condensed soup casseroles Rebecca doubtlessly prepared. What was going to happen to those poor children as they grew up with that terrible woman? Rebecca would probably outlive them all, wouldn't that be something?

Thank goodness Kelly and Andy were finally getting down to business. Would they have even started trying, had Ann-Marie not intervened and given Kelly a talk? She knew that these days, celebrities were having babies practically into their fifties, but Kelly was thirty-six and time was running out. When she was Kelly's age, Ann-Marie had two children in grade school already. No one wanted to put their baby at risks from Advanced Maternal Age. Everyone knew that there were all sorts of complications and developmental problems from women with older ovaries. Maybe she should have frozen her eggs?

"I'm just saying that since your dad passed away, I've been awfully lonely out here. And you're not getting any younger either, you know." Ann-Marie knew she was being manipulative; she was nothing if not self-aware. Sometimes with Kelly it didn't work if you told her that things were for her own good; she needed to understand how her decision fell into place in the larger sphere of the family.

"Eh, what's that? Speak up, young-un!" Kelly said in a squeaky old lady voice.

"Oh, honey, you know I'm just thinking of your well-being," Ann-Marie had said. "I don't want you to get all stressed about this; just relax and let nature takes its course. And if nature doesn't work, they have lots of ways to get people pregnant these days."

"Glad to hear your vote of confidence," Kelly had replied dryly.

Lately, their conversations had become strained. Ann-Marie knew that Kelly felt put-upon by her "nosy" mother. She was probably listening to Andy's mother for advice, and God knows what that woman was telling her. Ann-Marie remembered how Marjorie Gallagher had behaved at Andy and Kelly's wedding. She was so drunk she practically fell into the cake. Bo had laughed and called her the life of the party, but Ann-Marie had been livid. Marjorie was bossy and opinionated and loud. Thank God, she didn't live too nearby, but that almost didn't matter these days with smart phones and facetime and skype and all that nonsense.

Some girls listened to their mother's advice. Maybe Kelly was just not going to be one of those girls anymore. What if Ann-Marie ended up having a relationship with Kelly like she did with Sean? Now she was just sounding crazy. But really, this time she would have to be more firm with Kelly and tell her straight out that she was running out of time and needed to get down to business with this whole baby thing. It was bad enough that poor Bo would never get to see Kelly's children. Did Kelly want her own mother to miss out too, because that's where it sure seemed like it was heading.

Ann-Marie squinted and fumbled around for one of the several pairs of reading glasses she stowed throughout the house. She could've sworn she'd just seen her favorites, the cute red ones sitting on the arm of the rust-colored chair. Oh, well, Ann-

Marie fumbled around until she spotted her black-rimmed readers nestled in among the newspapers, and then tapped in the digits for Kelly's cellphone. The call went to voicemail. She ended the call, waited roughly three seconds, and called Kelly's number again.

"Hi, honey, it's just me, calling to say hi and see how you're doing. Give me a ring when you get a chance. Love you!"

Ann-Marie was willing to bet that Kelly had stopped off at one of those smoothie places that all the young people flocked to these days. She couldn't understand how Kelly could stand the taste of those icky things, made with soy and greens and all that other so-called healthy stuff. It "cleansed" her, Kelly had claimed.

Well, at any rate, Ann-Marie thought, Kelly would have to start eating healthier for the baby. And speaking of health, Ann-Marie grimaced as she swallowed a mouthful of the Raspberry Zing, now lukewarm. It did have a nice tangy flavor, but nothing beat a good cup of coffee. Her phone rang.

"Hey, Mom," it was Kelly.

"Well, there you are!" replied Ann-Marie. "Did you go to one of those Starbucks after class and get a soy something? I called you twice this morning already. Or was it traffic?"

"No. Well, I don't know." Kelly replied. "There might have been, but I didn't go this morning."

"Oh, well that's all for the best. I'm not much of a fan of that yoga stuff. I know it makes you feel better, and I know that Andy has been encouraging it for you, so I'm sure it has some health benefits. But really, taking a nice long walk might be even better for you. Have you thought of that? I know it's getting colder and colder these days, but once you get a good pace going, you warm up. I used to walk almost every day with your father."

"Ok,"

"Are you getting a cold, honey? You sound awfully congested."

"No, I'm. Mommy. I can't talk right now."

44

"Baby, what is it?" Ann-Marie suddenly found it difficult to breathe. Unbidden, a host of terrible scenarios flew into her consciousness. It must be Andy. He had hit Kelly. Or he had left her. Maybe Kelly had found out that he had a mistress. Or he had gambled away all their money. Maybe it was all lost in the stock market. Or Kelly could be sick.

Kelly's words came out in choking sobs, "I – we – we tried and we tried -- and I waited and then I took a pregnancy test and it – I was pregnant, and this morning I got up and" she broke off.

Ann-Marie closed her eyes. "Oh, honey, it happens. I'm so terribly sorry. It's horrible these tests that let you know so early; they get your hopes up so early when you otherwise wouldn't even have noticed. Please, don't worry. You're still so young and so healthy."

Kelly kept crying; Ann-Marie put on a smile and spoke briskly.

"All right, my dear. You just sit tight. You and I are going to go out to lunch today. Ok?" she said.

Kelly sniffled. "No, I'm alright. You don't need to come all the way out here."

"I'm your mother and I want to see my baby girl. You and I are going out to lunch. And maybe we'll get manicures afterwards." Ann-Marie's voice was firm.

"Ok," Kelly perked up a little.

"Now, that's the spirit! Hold tight and I'll see you in an hour."

Ann-Marie put down her mug and glanced outside the window. The lawn was sprinkled with brown oak leaves, as well as some of those tiny little honey locust leaves that were always such a pain in the rear to get with the rake. For crying out loud, she had finished the front clean just a half an hour ago. Maybe she would simply bite the bullet and get a lawn service like old Don Falco. She'd make sure to ask for the senior discount too. Ann-Marie changed out of her lawn-work "grubbies" and into a nice cashmere turtleneck and slacks. About ten minutes after she left the house, the phone in the kitchen rang.

"Hi, Ann-Marie, this is Sheila from Doctor McElroy's Office. We just wanted to call you to discuss the results of your biopsy. I'm happy to report that there were no irregularities or cancerous cells detected. We're going to keep watching you closely, though, so please call our office back and we'll schedule an appointment for six months from now."

Outside, Karen and Goose had continued down Chester Street, all the way to Idlewood Lane and the train stop, where Karen sat down on a faded green bench to examine her phone. Goose squatted on his haunches and sniffed at the air. Karen squinted at a notification, listened to her voicemail, nodding. She put her head in her hands for a moment, then looked helplessly at the dog.

"Oh, Goose, baby, how am I going to do this?" the dog looked at her gently. Karen could swear that Goose understood exactly she meant. "Help me through this, will you?" She scratched Goose's ears and he licked her hand. "Thanks, big guy." She called the number back.

"Hi, this is Karen Falco, Don's wife. Yes, Doctor North told me you folks would be in touch with me. Yes. Uh-huh. Yeah, it's been, well, you know. Fine, that would be fine. My daughter and grandson are coming around in a bit; you can meet them too. Thank you. Yes, of course, his being comfortable is what's most important. Thanks, we appreciate you folks coming out. It's very kind. I'll see you around one, then."

The woman and her dog got up and walked the rest of the way back home.

4. Left to Chance

She loved the *Godfather* films, well, one and two. Nobody liked three. She had minored in Film Studies at college with a senior thesis entitled: "The Politics of Sexual (Re)presentation in the Film Noirs of the 1940s" She also displayed an impressive knowledge of professional football (despite being a Patriots fan) and author Christopher Hitchens. She was thirty-five and single, never been married. She lived in Summit, New Jersey. Glenn, too, was away from home.

Glenn had arrived the prior afternoon at Sky Harbor Airport in Phoenix. The flight was excruciating, filled more than usual with babies unused to changing air pressure in the cabin. When he deplaned, there was a veritable fleet of wheelchairs waiting to be filled by older passengers in the jet bridge. That was the territory out here. Because during this visit Glenn was teaching a seminar, he had more luggage than usual. He hated to check bags, but what could you do? The firm was paying his travel expenses, so check away. As always when he arrived in the Valley of the Sun during winter months, the expansive blue sky was shocking in its brilliance.

Like every airport in every major city in the country, signs led the way to BAGGAGE CLAIM along windowed walkways. Sky Harbor had a nice southwestern flair, with zig-zagged, geometric patterns on the carpets and walls, and soft yellow, brown and pale blue hues evoking Native American artwork. It felt so good to get out of Whistler, and not just because the temperature in Arizona was fifty degrees higher than home. Glenn needed a break from home and routine; the conference could not have been scheduled at a better time.

A large shuttle bus carried travelers to the Rental Car Center, a sprawling structure about five minutes' drive from the airport. At the Hertz desk, Glenn filled out paperwork for his Toyota Prius. Ignoring the directions on the GPS to take the faster Highway 51 to his destination, Glenn drove North on 44th street. He liked to go past the red sandstone snout of Camelback Mountain at Echo Canyon Park. The tension in Glenn's neck and shoulders eased as the sun started to slip behind Lookout Mountain and Piestewa Peak, creating craggy purple silhouettes. One more turn and he arrived at the Camelback Inn, now known rather cumbersomely as the JW Marriott Camelback Inn and Spa.

He'd asked Paige to come along, knowing how much she loved Scottsdale. When the conference was held in New York, Charleston or Miami, Paige had begged off, but she always went when it was Scottsdale. She loved the saguaros and bougainvillea and the scent of sagebrush and creosote. This time, though, Paige had just blinked at Glenn when he asked if she wanted to come.

"Really," This was not a question.

"Paige – "

"No, thanks," she had smiled a bit after she spoke, maybe to make Glenn feel better, or maybe to bring an air of humanity to the pallid exchange. Then she left with the dog on yet another of her solitary walks.

Accountants were swarming on the Camelback Inn from all over the country. The somewhat bland title for this year's conference for financial planning CPAs was "Building the Future Today." Whiteboards throughout the lobby area advertised all the different activities, seminars and classes available over the next three days. Glenn had reserved a "casita" away from the main hotel area. These gatherings tended to be loud, especially closer to the bar and pool area at night.

Glenn checked in and checked all his emails, texts and voicemails. Just some of the usual nonsense. And as expected, not a word from Paige. Not that Glenn expected her to check up on him like a parent, but it would have been something just to have her ask if the flight was on time, or something as banal and meaningless as that. But Glenn wasn't about to hold his breath.

Ted Archer and Olivia Gregorian from the home office were already checked in, Glenn discovered via text messages. They were already at the Inn's lobby watering hole, Bar 1936, sampling bourbons. When Glenn stopped by their table, to Ted's whooping greeting, he was introduced to two other conference attendees.

"Glenn, meet Phil Young and Dorothy Dietrich. They're out of New York." Ted explained, grabbing an extra chair for Glenn. Ted was a bit shiny-faced from drinking.

"Ted, only a fool like you would come to Arizona and drink bourbon. Where's my tequila?" Glenn asked, eliciting further whoops from Ted.

"Glenn Whiteside, right?" the woman asked, extending her hand. She looked to be no more than thirty, with a broad smile and dark hair pulled back in a ponytail.

"Indeed," Glenn raised his eyebrows.

"I'll be introducing you tomorrow morning." She replied. "I thought you looked familiar; we've got photos of all the speakers in the program."

The five of them got into Glenn and Phil's rental cars and drove a bit up Lincoln to El Chorro, where they met other accountants at the rustic western-themed bar area and ate burgers. For numbers guys, they were a pretty fun bunch, Glenn admitted to himself. Dorothy had a great smile. A nice young gal.

Glenn was the keynote speaker a morning seminar entitled "Current Challenges and Key Risks in Financial Reporting" in the Palo Verde Boardroom. His head was only slightly pounding from all the margaritas the night before. Dorothy flashed her lovely smile at Glenn. She was dressed in a navy slacks and lavender blouse, with a navy blue and white polka dot scarf around her neck. Glenn thought she looked the perfect mixture of business-like and beautiful.

It wasn't until the post-seminar luncheon that Glenn discovered the less obvious, but no less attractive aspects to Dorothy Dietrich, not the least of which was her cache of *Godfather* quotes.

"I ain't no band leader," she deadpanned. "Yeah, I heard that story." And Glenn roared with laughter.

"Are you for real?" he asked, and Dorothy smiled that fantastic smile again.

At her age, Dorothy was only a little bit jaded; she could practically see the cogs turning in Glenn's brain as he chatted and, let's face it, flirted, with her. He was a nice looking man, though his grey hair probably made him look much older than he was. Glenn made no effort to hide his wedding ring either, Dorothy noticed. She found him to be an affable guy, much less of a pig than a lot of the men you meet at these sorts of events. Usually there were only two types: complete boors who slobbered on you, or guys who were super straight-laced, and only later did they start slobbering too.

Glenn struck her as the type of guy she'd like to actually date, if he didn't live across the country. Oh, yeah, and have a wife. Whatever little fantasy he was indulging by this time he spent with Dorothy, she was enjoying herself. What was so wrong with that? It was fun to talk about random stuff like the *Godfather* movies; it reminded her of talking to Eric.

She was not supposed to be thinking of Eric, Dorothy reminded herself. Hadn't she spent all those months in counseling precisely so that she could get over him? She needed to let Eric go; that's what Allyson, her shrink said. That's what her girlfriends all said; that's what her mother said. Eric was reckless and handsome; he laughed as much as he spoke. He wrote poetry and composed ballads that he played on his guitar. He wrote songs for her. God, she had been crazy for him.

"Exactly! Coppola has Pacino walking through a maze of darkened hospital hallways because he's starting his descent into darkness, his entry into the family business in that pivotal scene. It's a visual metaphor."

Dorothy was a hand-talker, Glenn noticed, but it added to her effervescent charm. They talked and laughed until afternoon slipped into early evening, and the buses arrived to take interested conference-goers on a tour of Taliesin West. Dorothy said she wanted to swim instead.

"I want to make everyone back home on the east coast jealous," she said. "I *have* to swim in February; those poor slobs back in New Jersey are freezing!"

It was a cool evening, but the pool was heated. Glenn had not even packed a bathing suit, so he sat on the edge of the pool and dangled his feet in the water. Dorothy splashed around for a few minutes, and asked Glenn to take a picture of her in the water; she then texted the picture to "the girls" back home and wrapped herself in a towel.

"Will you be going to the golf outing scheduled for tomorrow?" Glenn asked.

"Nah, I don't golf," Dorothy replied. "I'm going for a hike."

She wanted to climb Camelback Mountain, she said. She was not any kind of an athlete, so she would be taking the Cholla Trail, the longer but less difficult of the two paths to ascend Camelback. There were stairs cut into the stone in parts, and guardrails as well. It wasn't until you were almost at the top that you really needed to scramble on the rocks with your hands, she told him. It was a personal challenge, Dorothy admitted. She was terrified of heights.

51

"So this is some sort of bucket list for you?" Glenn asked. "That's really great. Good for you!"

She told him she'd tried to do it once before, the last time she's been in Scottsdale, in fact. But she hadn't made it all the way. This time, she said, she was going to do it.

"If you'd like, you're welcome to come with me. Give me your phone number. I'll shoot you a text when I'm ready to go." And the two exchanged numbers.

Once back in her room, Dorothy changed out of her wet bathing suit and into a pair of jeans and a sweatshirt. She wanted to walk through Old Town and pretend it was 2010 all over again, when she had come here with Eric for an impulsive long weekend getaway. They'd been dating each other a few months then, the honeymoon period of their relationship. Dorothy was starry-eyed and swoony, drunk with exhilaration and romance. Eric was an intellectual. He longed to teach Modern Poetry, but instead taught classes on Technical Writing at Union County College. Dorothy longed to take one of his classes, just to sit in the back of the class and listen to him talk. Eric had an oddly thin and slightly scratchy voice, with just the faintest hint of his Arizona roots in his vague twang. Eric was born in southern Utah, but had grown up in the Phoenix area. He was tall and rangy, maybe not quite movie-star handsome, but darned close to it. Dorothy called him her cowboy.

It had been April, and much hotter. Dorothy told Eric she wanted to go full-on tourist and do all the things one needed to do on a visit to Scottsdale. So, she bought a pair of boots at Gilbert Ortega, with Eric's grinning approval. He later surprised her with a turquoise and silver bracelet he bought at a tiny shop on Buckboard. Eric curled his long arm around Dorothy's shoulders, and steered them into the Rusty Spur Saloon, where they drank Buds and listened to honky-tonk. Because it was a Thursday, the local Art Walk was going on in Old Town. Palm trees were strung with Christmas lights and the numerous local art galleries stayed open late, most of them passing out small plastic cups of wine to visitors. Eric and Dorothy held hands and talked about David Foster Wallace novels and songs by Coldplay, while voices and laughter wafted over the canal from the restaurants near the big mall. Dorothy had felt bohemian and worldly. Sure, she worked at an accounting firm and was a boring numbers girl, but there she was in the Wild West with an incredibly sexy poet/professor. He knew the names of the cacti and those wild-looking desert trees ("they're called *palo verdes*").

They took a sunrise hike at Camelback Mountain; Eric chose the Cholla Trail, out of consideration for Dorothy's lack of climbing skills. At first, it had been fine: the trail was clear and sloped upward at an easy rate. She and Eric took photos of their progress at the switchbacks. Markers positioned every thirty feet or so kept them apprised of their progress. Then they reached the Saddle portion of the hike, a straightaway path on the side of the mountain, with a rock wall on one side and a steep drop-off on the other side. Dorothy had been frozen with what she knew was an irrational fear. Eric cajoled her, saying he'd stay on the drop-off side as they walked, but that made Dorothy terrified that he would fall and leave her there alone. Finally, she burst into tears and Eric comforted her as best they could as they scrambled back down the mountain.

"It's alright, baby," Eric murmured in her ear. "I'm here." And she had felt safe.

Ah, youth, Dorothy now thought wistfully. She and Eric had continued hot and heavy for a while. They started discussing the possibility of moving in together, but in the end Eric told Dorothy he didn't want to get committed. Dorothy had panicked; she told him it was alright, and they could just live together and be free spirits without any need for commitment. She just wanted to be with him. Eric smiled and told her that was a nice idea, but it would never work.

"Ok, then tell me what *will* work?" she had cried. "I want this to work; it can work!" He hadn't responded, just looked at her sadly.

Not long after, Eric stopped returning her calls and texts. In a spasm of madness, Dorothy drove down to Cranford, New Jersey one Friday morning, a day she knew he didn't teach, and parked down the street from Eric's apartment. She watched him leave, wearing his faded denim jacket and carrying his leather briefcase. Hating herself, she followed him to Lora's Tea Room on Centennial Avenue, where she spied on Eric as he sat drinking coffee and typing on his laptop for two hours. From a spot across the street, Dorothy could just barely see the curve of Eric's back, lit by the glow of his computer. Some shapes came near him, probably students saying hi, Dorothy guessed. When Eric left the tea room and got back into his aging Volkswagen Bug, he was not alone.

Dorothy went cold. She saw a woman around her age with short bobbed hair accompanying her man. They were holding hands. Because she apparently had to make her humiliation complete, Dorothy followed Eric and the woman back to his apartment. Then she drove back home to Summit and didn't leave her bed for three days.

It was her dear friend, Patti, who encouraged Dorothy to start seeing Allyson "to come to terms with things." Through her visits to Dr. Allyson Carr, Dorothy was able see that it wasn't that Eric wasn't ready to *commit*; he simply didn't want to commit to *her*. Yes, maybe he had lied, both to spare her feelings and to make himself seem more virtuous. Yes, you loved him, and he was wrong for you and now you have to pick the pieces back up. It had been an awful year or two. Dorothy had not quite picked herself up and dusted herself off, as the old song went, but she had not collapsed in a heap either. And now there was this nice older man, clearly interested in her, in this city synonymous with romance to Dorothy.

Tourists were milling around everywhere in Old Town, clogging the sidewalks. They clustered near the Sugar Bowl and Grimaldi's Pizza, taking pictures under the big cowboy sign. It was mid-season, the perfect time for snowbirds. You could tell the rookies from the locals by how many layers of clothing they wore. True Arizonans, or at least those who wanted to look the part, wore jeans and jackets, Eric had told her; it was the outsiders who wore shorts and tees. Dorothy smiled nostalgically, feeling worldly-wise in her Levis.

It was just a walk up a rock, Dorothy thought; it might be fun to hike with someone else. Frankly, given her phobia, it would be safer to hike with someone else. This Glenn person was funny and sweet. It was really just damned nice to feel pretty and desired again, if only by someone she would probably never see again. They wouldn't have to go all the way to the top. They could even stop before they got to the Saddle section.

Dorothy's phone buzzed. At first she didn't realize who the text was from; it was an unfamiliar number.

"Hey there, I'm going to get some golfing in tomorrow morning with Ted and the gang. Have a blast on your hike. Cheers, Glenn."

It was for the best, Dorothy knew. After all, she was no home-wrecker. The idea was ludicrous. Not that the hike would have meant anything more than a couple colleagues taking in the scenery during a professional conference. Nothing to see here, folks. She had been stupid to suggest he come along anyway. At any rate, now she didn't have to worry. Dorothy was shocked to find that she was getting a little weepy as she sat by a fountain with statues of running horses; she half-laughed, half-sniffed. Really? Is this what you're turning into? Just blame it on Old Town memories.

Ten minutes later, Dorothy pulled her rental back into the parking lot at the Camelback Inn. A nightcap at Bar 1936, you say? Don't mind if I do. The hotel bar was still crowded with conference attendees in various stages of drunkenness. Dorothy ordered herself a fresh lime margarita, the only kind of margarita you should ever order, Eric had told her once, unless you want people to think you're a tenderfoot. She scanned the crowd for anyone she knew, and spotted Fiona Walker, from the home office back in New York.

"Hey there, Fifi, how you doin'?" Dorothy called. Fiona's face lit up. She waved Dorothy over to her, spilling a little of her martini as she did so.

"Oh, honey," Fiona cried, swaying just a little, "I've been looking for you! There is this guy you just have to meet. He's from Philly and he's single and he's adorable."

Dorothy smiled. "Now that's an offer I can't refuse." And she let Fiona lead her over to the sandy-haired man with wire-rimmed glasses who was seated at the bar, nursing a beer.

Back in his casita, Glenn eased himself down onto the bed with a tiny bottle of bourbon from the minibar, turned on the television, and flipped through stations until he found a basketball game.

5. Reason Not the Need

Grace was not late. At least, not yet, but Amy got out a bottle of wine anyway. She may as well sit down quietly and weather the happy homecoming with a little help from the noble grape. It was Friday night, a week before Thanksgiving. Gracie still had classes at the high school on Monday and Tuesday next week, but the college students were returning back to the town of Whistler in droves. And guess whose daughter was seeing (not dating, Grace had repeated emphatically) a college boy? And not just any college boy, but a local boy, a former hometown hero on the basketball court, and charitable organizer who regularly got written up in the local paper.

Amy did not care about the boy's local pedigree; what bothered her was his age, two years older than her Gracie. Oh, be honest, the reason that boy made her toes curl up was because of the flowers. The mystery flowers. The "Why on earth would that boy have given you a huge bouquet of roses, huh, Grace?" flowers. Grace said it was nothing, and Amy didn't believe her.

And the fact that Amy didn't believe her own little girl was killing her. She and Grace were becoming strangers.

She asked Scott if he wanted any wine, but he declined, so Amy only got one glass out of the cupboard. Scott's prized "World's Greatest Dad" coffee mug squatted in there, front and center, as if announcing: "did you notice that I'm the only one of my kind?" Rest assured, Amy noticed. The mug was several years old; Grace hadn't wanted to give Amy a prize back in her middle school days, and she surely wasn't going to do so as a high schooler.

Ever since Gracie began high school three and half years ago, she effectively began to reinvent herself as a rebel. Gone were the pastels and the unicorns and the bubble-gum lip gloss; she started wearing only black clothing, distressed jeans and baggy tee shirts or hoodies. Instead of listening to the soundtrack from *Wicked*, she listened to Eminem and Chance the Rapper. It was disconcerting to Amy, who naively associated dark clothing and rap music with antisocial behavior. It was nice, however, Amy admitted, that Grace didn't strut around half naked like many of her friends did.

"What friends, *Mother*?" Grace would intone, giving her a look.

Amy's mind raced for an example. "Well, Nellie, and Isadora. I saw them the other day going into Starbucks."

"I literally haven't spoken to them in about two years. Nice try, though." And Grace disappeared into her room.

During her freshman year at Whistler High School, Grace had told Amy she no longer wanted to be enrolled in ballet or soccer. She bought a skateboard (an oddly retro item, in Amy's opinion); she started keeping a journal that she would hunch over and jot notes into, while looking around suspiciously; she sported a camouflage jacket she'd picked up at Goodwill. She did wear make-up, but only thick black eyeliner.

Even more disturbing to Amy was that Grace also renounced the group of friends with whom she'd been inseparable since Second Grade at Washington Elementary. And now, in Grace's final year at home, to add a soupcon of migraine to Amy's already formidable stress headache, Grace was seeing a college boy. Amy settled herself down with a pinot noir (Erath, Willamette Valley Estate, 2014) and prepared for a bumpy night. It was only eight-thirty and Grace's curfew was midnight. But since Ted was back in town this week, all bets were off.

Grace's own college selection was similarly up in the air. When Amy asked her daughter what she was looking for in higher education, Grace invariably rolled her eyes and said, "I don't care. Just not here." Scott made more mileage with their girl; she confessed to her father a desire to pursue studies in International Human Rights and Global Outreach.

"Can people really even *do* that?" Amy asked Scott.

"Of course they can -- and do," Scott acknowledged. "We call such people unemployed." Nevertheless, he encouraged Grace to follow her passion, so the family visited Indiana University at Bloomington and University of California at San Diego, among several other institutions, to check out their programs. Amy was completely dismayed at the idea of Grace attending college across the country, so she employed reverse psychology: talking up UCSD over IU, knowing Grace would prefer whichever school Amy disliked more. Applications were out and the waiting game began. Grace seemed nonplussed by the whole process, while Amy was a wreck of anticipation.

Ted, on the other hand, attended a tiny liberal arts college somewhere in Wisconsin, playing basketball. Amy doubted that Grace would follow the boy to a small school in the middle of nowhere, but her girl had been surprising lately. Anyway, Grace swore that the boy was Not Her Boyfriend, Scott pointed out, so why get upset about something that hasn't even happened yet? That was easy for Scott to say.

Amy sipped her pinot. Scott always had some chirpy little solution to problems, which was probably why he had been given the auspicious World's Greatest Dad mug, while Amy got shouting and tears and slammed doors. Scott couldn't understand the complicated noose of emotions and nerve-endings that was the bond between mother and daughter. When you have a little girl, Amy thought, you have to simultaneously recreate your own mother, yourself, and what you imagine for your daughter within her. It was a constant process of tearing down and putting up between the two. It was both atonement for Amy's mother, and hope for whoever Grace's children would be. It was a taut balance of keeping silent and speaking out; it was frankly exhausting. A girl has freedom to adore her father because he will always fundamentally remain an Other. But your Mom is *you*, warts and all. You become your own reflection of all the places your own mother fell short, and what you want to become. The balancing act can be unbearable.

Though they had been inseparable for the first twelve years of Grace's life, adolescence began a rift between Amy and her daughter. The sweet, dark-haired little cherub whom shopkeepers and total strangers referred to as Amy's "mini me" transformed overnight into a sulky, glowering changeling, who refused to wear the matching Christmas sweaters anymore and pulled away when Amy attempted to hug her. Admonishments as banal as "wash your face" led to seemingly days of sulking, with increasingly scraggly hair blocking Grace's eyes.

For dinner tonight, Amy had prepared a chicken pot pie from scratch, with extra carrots because she knew Grace loved them. They were one of the few hold-overs from Gracie's past that she still acknowledged as her own. Amy rolled out the pie crust, hoping that the pie might spark the reappearance of Grace's former dazzling smile. She would be so touched, wouldn't she, to know that Amy had cared enough to prepare one of her favorite meals for her? But of course Amy's phone had buzzed to notify Amy that Grace wouldn't be joining them for dinner that night. Her message a breezy: "sry going out with ted."

Amy was tempted to throw the still-unbaked pot pie in the garbage disposal, which of course would be completely childish, but would give Amy some temporary, albeit petty, satisfaction. Instead, she took a picture of the finished pie and texted it to Grace, admitting to herself that it was rather a passive-aggressive gesture. At any rate, Amy didn't care; the pie looked and smelled fantastic. Her daughter's reply was a disappointing: "Yum"

An abandoned can of Diet Coke sweated a ring of moisture onto the cherry wood veneer of the coffee table. A bit of detritus left by Hurricane Grace earlier in the day.

"Couldn't she at least have picked up some of this crap before she left?" Amy asked irritably.

"Maybe she'll finish it later," said Scott.

"You wanna put money on that?"

"Hey, they got that Park District Building built: miracles can happen in Whistler."

"I think she's getting bad habits from hanging out with that Ted."

In Amy's opinion, Ted had made too obvious of an effort to be cordial and smooth when Grace had introduced him to her and Scott last summer. "No worries, ma'am," the boy had smiled on their first date back in June. "We are off to be basic Millennials. Grace and I promise to consume our weight in kale and file petitions against traditional binary notions of gendered identity and selfhood." Grace had doubled over laughing.

After the two of them had left, Scott had chuckled, "Smart kid."

"Did you notice that he has some sort of a tattoo?" Amy mentioned, watching them drive off.

It was consistently irksome to Amy that Scott always seemed to understand Grace better. He always found an excuse for her behavior, and these days more often sided with Grace during her and Amy's increasingly frequent disagreements. On the rare occasion that he did reprimand Grace (like the time when she had used language so shocking that even-keeled Scott had exploded in anger), Grace had crumpled into a mask of woe, her brown eyes welling with tears. Scott had been helpless to continue his rage.

With her mother, on the other hand, Grace had perfected a pugilistic stance of defiance, her small chin lifted, mouth in a line. Grace did not cry before Amy's wrath. She inhaled it and spat it away with a smirk. It didn't seem to touch her, a tactic that infuriated Amy, who would never have dared to act that way in front of her own mother, a woman whose memory she repeatedly tried to revise or polish, and who now existed only to be compared against.

Amy grew up on the far southern tip of the state, in a town called Hogarth. Her family, the Waynes, had worked in the area's coalmines two generations ago, living hard and dying before their time. Then a manufacturing plant that had been a small source of jobs in the area, expanded its operations. It expanded from a small research center to one of the company's major Midwestern hubs, manufacturing washers, dryers and dishwashers. Proximity to rail lines and interstate highways soon made the plant grow to be the region's major employer.

Over the next few years, almost twenty percent of Hogarth's population was employed in some capacity at the factory, and the tiny town boomed from a population of 2,800 in 1970 to 4,400 by 1984. Her father, Douglas Wayne, was a Manager of Supplies and Logistics there. Her mother, Noreen, headed the workforce at the Customer Experience Center. Amy's big brother Don planned to study engineering at the state university when he graduated from high school, hoping to someday land one of the upper echelon jobs at the factory.

Almost as suddenly as the plant had expanded, corporate spokespeople announced that they would be closing the factory outside of Hogarth and moving their manufacturing branch overseas. The resulting layoffs hit every family in Hogarth, including the Waynes. Noreen kept her job, but Douglas was laid off. Don applied for an army ROTC scholarship for college, but was turned down. He attended, instead, the community college in Belmont, nearby, and worked part-time at the Harrah's casino as a server, with the revised goal of working his way up to becoming a craps dealer.

Hogarth began to crumble before Amy's eyes. People moved away, businesses closed, hope died. No one really blamed Douglas when his drinking got out of control. Amy Leigh Wayne entered high school as the bottom dropped out of her family. Noreen was clearly worried about her husband, but was powerless to stop him from his binges. To avoid going home to an increasingly self-loathing and violent father, Amy spent long hours after school studying. Her excellent grades and essays won her a prize from the Hogarth Rotary Club. Amy was also practical-minded. She researched scholarships at the library, and applied for as many as she could reasonably be considered for. Her hard work paid off; Amy was awarded a combination of merit and low-income scholarships to attend the big state university.

Ever-practical, Amy majored in Business, graduated with honors and moved to the city up North. She found an apartment, a roommate (the sister of a former classmate), and a job at H & R Block. She had just started her second year in the city when her brother Don called to tell her that both their parents were dead. Amy learned that it was, as she had expected for years, a drunk driving accident. As the details emerged, though, she discovered that Noreen had been driving and sober; she'd come to pick up Doug at a tavern when he couldn't make it home himself. The culprit was in the other vehicle, and was himself another casualty of the plant's layoffs.

Amy met Scott Miller on the bus in the rain. She laughed to friends later that, if she had viewed the scene in a movie, she would have dismissed it as overly cute and unrealistic. Scott had, in fact, flirted with Amy when she accidentally dripped onto his briefcase and files. "The least you can do," Scott told her, "is buy me a coffee."

He worked in Human Resources at some financial company in the city. Like Amy, Scott was practical, but with more of a twinkle in his eye and breezy outlook on life, which came from growing up in the affluent Eastern suburbs, Amy suspected. Scott Miller was, in fact, antithetical to most of Amy's experience, but in the best possible way.

They dated, courted, married and moved to suburbia, feathering their nest in the suburb of Whistler, with its sought-after school districts and enviable property values. The Millers bought a charming three-story Nantucket style home, and settled down to life with a landscaper and a cleaning lady every other week. Neither could wait to start their new family.

Amy continued working until she neared her due-date. And finally, after less than an hour of actual pushing, she had amazing Grace, a saving Grace, her Grace note. Amy barely noticed anyone's existence besides her new little girl. Motherhood made her glorious. Amy reveled in her dark-haired baby; she couldn't stop staring at the miracle she and Scott brought home from the hospital, sleepy and delicate. Amy catalogued her daughter's every move on page and on film: every hour Grace slept, every centimeter she grew, and the number of words in her infant vocabulary of sounds. The two looked very much alike, with thin brown hair, narrow foreheads and olive toned skin. Scott would joke that the two were sisters. Friends would buy the two matching outfits.

With every activity in which Grace was engaged, from Mandarin lessons to internet coding, Amy reminded herself of her own debt- and despair-ridden childhood. She would be there for Grace, and give her anything she wanted. They weren't precisely rich, but they were worlds away from the struggles of Hogarth. Amy defined herself against her past.

As Grace grew older, and her dimpled knees became knobby and scabbed, she became more wary of Amy's effusiveness. She started to rankle when Amy bought them matching sweaters for holidays. In defiance of Amy's elaborate ritual of braiding her hair, Grace insisted on wearing it loose and uncombed, resulting in almost comic screaming matches. Grace blundered into adolescence with an alarming (to Amy) degree of sullenness and sarcasm.

Grace pretended to her mother that her own puberty did not occur, refusing to reach out to her for any advice or commiseration. Amy's own entry into adolescence had been an exercise in mortification, with Noreen always busy working and taking care of Douglas, relying on Amy's resilience and practicality. For her own daughter, Amy planned ahead; she bought First Period Survival Kits, filled with "adorable" calendars, pads, and chocolates. This, she thought, at least is a situation in which every girl wants her mom. But Grace had reacted with horror, scowling at Amy, running to her room and slamming her door.

Her friends' experience appeared to be much different than Amy's was.

"My Riley couldn't wait to put the Period Tracker app on her phone!" beamed Amy's friend, Kathleen, a mother of Grace's classmate. "She loves knowing how many days are left so she can plan her wardrobe. Kids these days will enjoy anything if it comes with an app."

Except, apparently, for Grace. Generally frowning, forehead marred by rashes of angry red pimples, Grace sulked around in her shapeless black tee shirts and high-top Chuck Taylor sneakers. Her clothing was specifically chosen to hide any sign of her gender. When Amy suggested that Grace might want to wear something a little brighter for once, Grace exploded with, "Ok, fine, I get it. I'm hideously ugly and all my clothes suck. Thanks a ton, Mom. I'm terribly sorry to be such a disappointment."

Was it that Grace was an only child? She and Scott had attempted for years to increase their family, but no sibling resulted. "We couldn't do any better than you, honey." Scott would say. He always knew what to say to Grace to get her to smile when Amy clearly did not.

For Father's Day several years ago, Grace had gotten Scott the "World's Greatest Dad" coffee mug. "I'll be getting mine next Mother's Day, right?" Amy had joked.

"Sure, Mom." Grace had said, ducking into the powder room and sliding the pocket door closed behind her. Amy couldn't tell if Grace was being sarcastic or truthful, though she suspected the former. And indeed, as time went on, Amy had never received a mug, though she had gotten an allotment of Hallmark cards.

Some girls are just more naturally Daddy's girls, Amy thought. And it was wonderful that Gracie had a strong father figure, unlike the childhood Amy had endured, which grew more and more elaborately desolate and disappointing in her memory the longer Amy thought about it.

It was now 9:30. Scott was already reading in bed. Amy was two glasses into her bottle of pinot noir. She flipped channels on the television fiercely, indignant that Grace would not love her as much as she deserved and ashamed of herself for feeling that way. Noreen could never wait up for Amy to come home. She worked too many shifts. Amy, however, had cleared her plate for Grace. But it didn't seem to matter.

"You know kids don't like to be pushed too much," Scott had warned once. "You know she's acting up towards you because she needs you."

Amy sipped her wine. They had made it through the prickly, awkward early adolescent days, and now Grace was on the verge of going to college. Her baby needed her before she went away forever, just like Amy had needed Noreen. Maybe that was the problem all along. Grace just didn't know how to articulate it.

Tears welled up in Amy's eyes. If only Grace weren't out with Ted, her "friend" ("Oh, my God, Mother, how can you even think he is my boyfriend?"). Fine, at least he was a local Whistler boy, but he had some connection to that big story about the local kid a couple years ago, which had left the whole town shaken. Grace had not known Ted personally then, but she and her friends had spent days talking and texting about the situation. Grace probably thought of him as some sort of outreach mission project.

But then again, there had been the flowers. Grace had begun her friendship (if that was all it was) with Ted shortly after school let out last summer. At first it had been text and facetime based, but by July, they were meeting out by Bartleby Park or going to Otis Pond behind the new Park District building. Not long before Ted was readying to return to his sophomore year, the Whistler Flower Shoppe delivered a green glass vase of a dozen long-stemmed pink roses to Grace, with the accompanying note reading baldly, "Thank you."

Grace read the note, shrugged, and took the vase upstairs to her room. Amy, on the other hand, could barely contain her rage. Obviously, they were sleeping together, and that pig wanted her to stay faithful to him, so he made a great show of being romantic. Grace was barely eighteen! "He is a college student, she's still in high school and he's *thanking* her for screwing him," Amy wailed.

"Can you blame him?" Scott had sensibly answered. "Look, at least he cares enough about her to thank her." When Amy started to sputter, Scott added, "Kids are going to have sex, whether we want them to or not. At least we know that Grace is a smart girl who feels comfortable talking to her parents about what's going on in her life."

"Maybe to you," Amy spat. "She never says shit to me."

"Don't be that mom, Amy." Scott returned. "You don't want to be *that* mom." He went back to playing poker on his phone, leaving Amy to stew. When she later asked Grace about the flowers and cryptic note, her daughter shrugged.

"We had a long talk," Grace offered.

"And that's it?"

Grace's eyes narrowed. "What more do you want? A transcript perhaps?"

"Don't you think it's a little bit odd when someone who's just a *friend* gives you a dozen roses?" Amy said.

"What exactly are you implying, Mother?" Grace was stiffening with rage. "Is it so difficult for you to imagine that anyone might want to be nice to me? After all, I'm wearing a baggy shirt, as you always like to point out."

The conversation had declined from there.

When Ted asked Grace whether she wanted to get together this evening, Grace had immediately called up Sally Bundren and cancelled her babysitting gig for that night, to Amy's great displeasure. At least, to Gracie's credit, she also gave Sally the numbers of a couple friends who could possibly fill in for her. Poor Sally Bundren has sounded desolate in a voicemail she left on the Miller's landline, requesting to know Grace's availability in coming weeks.

"She sounded like she was about to cry," Amy explained to Grace. "Are you sure you want to break this?"

Grace rolled her eyes, "Mrs. Bundren's always like that. She needs to chill." Amy didn't argue, though she wanted to. Sally did seem like she has a screw loose somewhere. Her girls were awfully cute, though.

Amy was tired of battling her little girl. She needed to act more like a mother and less like a combatant. Grace was the way she was because Amy had let her do whatever she wanted all her life, which was the exact opposite of how Amy had grown up. Why then, was Amy acting surprised that Grace was, in fact, not behaving at all like she had at Grace's age? Wasn't that what Amy had wanted for her baby after all? Wasn't that the whole point of letting her find her own way? Jesus, she really had this parenting thing down, didn't she?

As she sipped the last of the wine, Amy decided she was going to be a better mother to her beautiful little girl, in her final months as a high schooler. She'd tell her baby how proud she was of her, how much she loved her. And that these stupid fights they sometimes had were frankly luxuries when you thought about them, right? Grace could marry Ted, if he was the guy she loved; Amy would happily dance at their wedding and welcome Ted into the family if Grace loved him. Grace's happiness mattered more than anything. Amy's eyes leaked sentimental, pinot noir-laced tears. How unbelievably proud she was of her sweet baby, her little mini me. Maybe Scott was the World's Greatest Dad, but that didn't mean that Grace wasn't Amy's own special girl.

A thud of footsteps on the porch and suddenly Grace stood in the foyer, her cheeks pink from the cold. Amy put down her wineglass and frowned.

"Oh! Grace, sweetie, you're home already?"

"Um, yeah,"

"It's barely ten," Amy stammered, "is everything ok?"

"Oh, man, this is the *best*!" Grace responded. "I come back *early*, just to *appease* you, and the first thing you do is give me shit?"

"Do you want to talk about anything, honey?"

"Like what?" Grace was squared off and ready for a fight.

"Nothing, sweetie. I hope you had a good time."

Grace pounded up the stairs, producing much more noise than one would think possible for a girl of her slim build. Amy heard her daughter say goodnight to Scott before she closed the door to her room.

6. "Whan That Aprill"

One of the first things people learned about the town of Whistler was that it was ideal for commuters. Realtors touted the "dreamy" fifteen minute train-ride into the city, as well as the number of nonstops available, to potential clients. It was a big selling point. Although Whistler was a small village, its length ran along the commuter rail line into the city. Residents had a choice of two stops: Downtown Whistler at Main Street, or the Idlewood Lane stop on the North Side.

Most passengers boarded at Main Street, and as a result, more trains stopped there. The Main Street Station was constructed of weathered red brick, with a rooftop of cedar shingles. Inside the air-conditioned facility, one could purchase tickets or pick up a train schedule at a service window; restrooms were located at the far south side of the structure. The Whistler News-Stop, a kiosk offering commuters local papers, as well as issue of *The Wall Street Journal* and *The New York Times* and some magazines, hunched in the corner of the station's South end. The Main Street Café, a tiny establishment selling pastries, coffee, and sandwiches, occupied the North side.

In contrast, the Idlewood Lane stop was barely more than a crossing with small pavilions offering shelter from the elements on either side of the tracks. A wooden sign, visible from the tracks, read "Idlewood Lane" in faux rustic lettering. A coin-operated newspaper vending machine stood next to the pavilion, selling copies of *The Whistler Chronicle* for a dollar.

This morning, it threatened rain. About two dozen commuters spread themselves out along the train platform. It was a grey day with little wind, and the air was damp, near fifty. Most of the travelers were white, male and over thirty-five, not a surprising demographic for the area. The women who stood there were all uniformly well-dressed, with sensible, yet colorful, Hunter boots in anticipation of a looming shower. The 7:17 train was running late.

Scott nodded to Jonathon Zeigler as he approached the Idlewood Lane stop. "Rainy days and Mondays, huh?"

"You got that right," Jonathon responded curtly.

"Good weekend?" he asked politely.

Jonathon shrugged, "Eh, too short." He went back to looking at his phone.

Hal tried to fold his *New York Times* in an easily readable fashion. To his dismay, the pages flapped loudly and he wasn't quite able to get the crease working. He tried it again, but the paper refused to cooperate. He noticed a woman looking at him irritably as the paper crunched. Hal grinned sheepishly and shrugged his shoulders.

"I swear, I'll get it to work in a minute," he laughed. "Pain in the ass, huh?"

"That's why I read my news online," the woman said.

"I like the old fashioned way," Hal remarked. "Though it doesn't like me, at least not today." He crushed the paper down into the semblance of a fold at last. "Ah, that'll do!"

Once Hal turned away, Lauren stopped smiling and rolled her eyes. She really wasn't in the mood for the train to be late today; her nose was running. Stupid spring always ended up wreaking havoc on her sinuses. She dug through her purse for some Kleenex. If this train didn't get here soon, she'd be out of tissue, great. Her head was so cloudy she couldn't even remember if she'd taken the Sudafed she'd left out on the counter. The weekend had been a congested, stuffy mess; it had broken Lauren's heart, but she'd had to bail from the Girls' Night Out with Cathy and Heather on Saturday. What was the point of drinking mojitos and cosmos like a college girl if you couldn't enjoy them? Why was it she seemed only to get sick when Jim had the kids for the weekend? That was a dirty trick. What if she took another Sudafed? If she had, in fact, already taken one, would an extra dose make her heart start racing, or whatever horror stories they now pedaled about the drug? These days, you couldn't even buy the stuff without showing your Driver's License to the pharmacist. Lauren liked to think of herself as liberal, but was there really any danger of someone like her cooking up crystal meth with a 24 pill packet of nasal decongestant?

If everything else was going to suck, at least Lauren was wearing her magic pants today, the black pants that made her rear end disappear. She tended to drag them out of the closet when she felt lousy because nothing can perk you up like knowing you look snazzy. Even better, her green and grey color block top was clean, so her outfit simply *worked*. Her daughter Ashley would have been self-righteously indignant, had she known what Lauren was thinking. Ashley was almost sixteen, and a co-founder of the High School's Gender Identity Club. She and her friends knitted pink caps and marched for equality under the law; Lauren applauded Ashley's efforts (and marched with her!), but simply could not get her daughter to appreciate the sheer joy of having a color-coordinated work outfit when your spirits were down.

Michael glanced around the train platform dismissively. Everyone here seemed old and boring. Their raincoats were uniformly khaki and their hair (on the men) was uniformly short and balding. If nothing else, he felt dark (Michael's coat and pants were black) and hairy. And, let's face it, Jewish. He might as well be wearing a glowing yarmulke he stuck out so much. It wasn't that he or Jackie practiced their faith; they were really only Jewish on High Holidays, and then more for the social aspect than any deep religious bond. The twins were not going to get any special religious education. Nevertheless, Michael felt a distance from his pallid fellow commuters that went beyond the mere fact of being new to Whistler.

They could have bought a home in the Northern suburbs, home to a considerably larger Jewish population. But his commute would have been longer, the available houses a bit smaller, and the schools less exceptional than Whistler. When you thought about it, after all, everybody starts out as a stranger at some point. Michael just wished it didn't quite seem so profoundly flavorless here in the Eastern 'burbs. Oh, people were friendly, sure. But would it kill them to build a decent deli anywhere within fifteen miles of Whistler? Hell, forget about deli; you couldn't even get edible pizza here in the Midwest. What kind of idiots thought deep dish was a good idea?

Neel Banerjee wheeled his carry-on luggage to the platform. He would be taking a flight this afternoon. Another trip to Atlanta. He hated the weather, hated the airport, hated the accents the people spoke with, and really hated the fact that nobody could seem to understand his soft East Indian accent. Neel did enjoy the sweet tea, though. It made his endless trips into Hartsfield somewhat bearable. He was heading the build-out for First Data's global e-commerce division, in the area of wireless point of sale devices. The end result would be quite satisfying, but for now, Neel wished all his meetings could be conducted virtually, rather than requiring his constant trips to Georgia. He took a gulp from his Starbucks travel mug and grimaced. Why on earth had he let Kara convince him that caffeine-free coffee was a viable option? What, really, was the point of coffee aside from the caffeine? Frankly, he'd rather have hot tea, but all of his business associates at First Data drank coffee and Neel was determined to be seen as just one of the guys. He smiled ruefully; that he would be seen as one of the guys among the Atlanta contingency, who spoke extra slowly to Neel to ensure that he could understand them, was about as likely as the build-out project finishing up this month.

"Hal!" cried an elaborately made-up woman wearing an Aquascutum raincoat, "I heard the big news; aren't you just so excited?"

"Oh, yeah," he smiled. "Thanks, Hannah. It's been a bit of a whirlwind, but we're getting used to the idea of it now."

"When you're father of the groom, you can just enjoy. It's the bride's family that does all the work." Hannah said.

"Don't say that to Joyce, ha-ha." They both laughed.

Scott Miller sighed and smiled tightly. Today was going to be a shit show. As head of Human Resources, he had to bring in an eighteen year employee of the firm, let's just call him Joe, and explain to him that his constant surfing of pornographic sights on the Internet was an unacceptable practice that violated their corporate policy. Moreover, Scott had a statement composed by Joe's executive assistant, Tonya, attesting that Joe had *shown* her some of the photographs from the sites, and asked her opinion on them. More than a trifle shaken, Tonya had called Scott in HR.

Everyone knew that Joe had recently undergone a rather messy (is there any other kind?) divorce, and had sort of lost it lately. Nathan Lin, the founder of Matterhorn Financial and a longtime pal of Joe's, had asked Scott to "see what Joe wants to do; maybe it's just retirement time?" The plan was for Scott to gently suggest to Joe that he retire. But the signs Scott was getting, after asking around on the fifteenth floor where Joe's office was located, was that Joe had no intention of leaving quietly. Tonya, for her part, indicated that she was planning on filing a complaint if Joe was not removed from the office pronto.

This was the sort of stuff that people always guessed went on in HR departments, but no one wanted to deal with: the office bad boy getting busted. They'd been on a streak for a year or so, with nothing more explosive than a couple employees leaving on disability and one guy all bent out of shape because of their group insurance plan. That sort of stuff was pretty basic. But this mess could potentially be catastrophic for all kinds of people.

Scott liked Joe. He was a good guy. Or at least, Scott had never seen Joe do anything disagreeable in his presence. He really had no *relationship* to the guy at all, merely one cog among many in a large-ish company that spanned several floors of their building and five satellite offices nationwide. Sometimes they saw each other coming in and out of the gym located on the building's lower level. Joe was always a pleasant, always ready with a joke. He remembered little things, like the name of Scott's wife and daughter, always asking after them. A Human Resources Director had to be brutal, though. Nobody wanted negative PR about man abusing his workplace privileges and demeaning women. It was becoming cliché, and it was not going to happen on Scott's watch. The next thing you knew, they'd have a reporter there investigating sexual harassment in the workplace and they'd all be on local tv.

"Kristy, how are you?" Glenn asked a red-haired woman wearing a Burberry trench-coat.

"Hey, Glenn, good to see you." She responded. She smiled brightly and touched Glenn's forearm.

"I wanted to thank you for all the help you gave us organizing things the other day." Glenn said, drawing nearer to her. "That really helped the project out tremendously. It's been, um, it's been challenging."

"Oh, don't mention it."

"Really, I just wanted to thank you. And tell you that it meant the world to me. And Paige too, of course. Both of us." He stumbled a bit.

"Oh, it was my pleasure, Glenn," she smiled. "Really, don't even mention it."

She was beginning to feel embarrassed, so Kristy pretended to look down at something on her phone. She didn't want to engage in small talk right now; she had to coordinate the Team Building Workshop at lunch. If the stupid train didn't get here pretty soon, she wouldn't have much time to go over the entire Power Point presentation. Kristy hated to run events on the fly; she liked precision and preparation. This day was not starting out well. As if to admonish her for pretending to use the phone as an excuse, her phone buzzed.

"Sadie, I told you that I can't take you to Tae Kwan Do after school; I'm going in to the office today. Mrs. Greene is taking you with Maggie. I don't care. No, that doesn't matter. You'll just have to work things out between the two of you. Are you kidding me, who cares? Work it out; you two need to deal with this on your own. I can't. Sorry, I can't."

Glenn, who had observed Kristy's conversation with a slight smile, turned away. He noticed Jason running up to the stop, as if he had sprinted all the way from home. When he neared the Idlewood crossing, Jason paused and stared at the crowd of people standing on the platform waiting. He looked perplexed, as well as tired; he was on his cell.

"So it's late?" he mouthed to Glenn, when clearly there was no train was forthcoming. Glenn looked at him, shrugged, and nodded.

"They had an announcement a while ago about a switching problem further on down the line, and it's backing up everything today." Glenn explained.

Jason made a face and then went back on the phone with IT. He was in the process of trouble-shooting; he needed Craig to log-on as Admin to the system and unlock his account because Paul Schneider had forgotten his password again. Yes, again. I don't know why he keeps forgetting either. Mr. Paul Schneider couldn't be bothered to call the IT Help Desk directly. No, Paul went through Jason because good ole Jason was always reliable. And probably because Paul couldn't remember how to get in touch with the Help Desk. Great.

A gift, that's it, she'd get them a little something, Shannon thought. She'd run out to Williams-Sonoma at lunch; Joyce mentioned that the kids were registered there. But do you get things off the registry as an engagement gift? Maybe she

76

should just go to Bloomingdale's and pick up a few Waterford tumblers? Everybody loved getting Waterford. Shannon had to make this present a big deal; they was the first of the kids of their little gang to get married. Shannon had always thought that the older brother would get hitched first, but that younger one had always been the crazier one, even way back when those boys were just little guys riding around on their Schwinns. Joyce was holding up beautifully, all things considered. If it had been Shannon's children, she'd be singing a different tune, of course. Then again, Sophie was still in college and Mark was too busy studying for the Bar Exam to be involved with anybody. Or was Shannon kidding herself? What about that girl Mark had mentioned, the one in his study group? Surely he wasn't really serious about her, was he? Shannon said a silent prayer for strength.

Dr. John Bolger was worried. Not about work; business was great, thank you very much. But about his old fraternity brother and lifelong friend, Murray. Murray wanted John to invest in his latest business venture, a chain of chiropractic clinics. He wanted $50,000 to start. This was a terrific investment; it was going to grow like crazy over a very short period, Murray promised. He had several of their other brothers from Lambda Chi participate in this investment opportunity. But something smelled funny to John. Something smacked of shady dealings.

"Never buy anything from a guy who's out of breath," John's father, the late great Martin Bolger had often said. And it certainly seemed like Murray was panting. They were meeting for lunch "just to catch up," but really so that Murray could try to sweet-talk John into investing. Maybe John should cancel. All he had to do was tell Murray that he had an emergency surgery to perform or something. Maybe he'd make a joke about the surgery to give it verisimilitude when he told Murray. John had a wide array of off-color urology jokes in his repertoire.

Jonathon Zeigler rubbed his eyes before reading the lengthy email message he had recently received from his mother.

She was asking why had it been such a long time since he and Martha brought the kids out to see them? Didn't he realize that his father wasn't getting any younger? And Jonathon knew that the Parkinson's was making it so hard for Dad to get around these days. You'd think that a mother wouldn't have to tell her own son that she'd like to see her sweet grandchildren before she got too old to enjoy them. Or was it that wife of his? I'll bet that you see her family all the time, don't you? Those Finleys can spend time with their grandchildren, but we apparently don't rate as highly in your estimation. Well, I guess that's the way it's going to be from now on, isn't it?

A tired-looking but ebullient man in rumpled khakis and a fleece half-zip sweater leaped into the midst of all the bored and irritated commuters. He had an impressive head of red hair sticking out in odd patches, as if he had slept on it, and carried a large paper bag that he shuffled through noisily.

"Alrighty, folks," he bellowed. "It's been a helluva last four days, but last night my mother-in-law arrived to save the day, so now I can finally celebrate: It's a Girl!" And he passed out handfuls of pink foil-wrapped chocolate cigars to the amusement of all.

"Congratulations," Jonathon grinned. The waiting commuters gathered round him; a few applauded. Several cooed as he displayed a few photographs on his phone, and shook his hand.

"Seven pounds, six ounces. Clara. She's our second girl. I can't believe it: two girls!"

Lauren patted the exuberant father on the shoulder, smiling indulgently. Guys like this one were the living example of what had been wrong about Jim. This guy here was so excited about his baby being born that he was making a fool of himself on a flipping train platform. That was more enthusiasm than Jim Steiner showed during the *entire twelve years* of their marriage. No, Lauren took it back: Jim had been very passionate when it came to the issue contributing any child support. Suddenly, he came to life on that issue. And now he had the nerve to introduce

Ashley and Brandon to that woman (who looked she could practically be his *daughter* from the photo the kids had showed her-- what the hell was he thinking?) Jim was "dating" now. Lauren sniffled and dug around for another tissue, but now they were all used, wadded up at the depths of her purse.

An automated voice boomed from the loudspeaker overhead: "Attention, an incoming train will be arriving in two minutes. Thank you for your patience during the delay." The commuters cheered again, and began spreading themselves out along the Idlewood Lane platform. After a few seconds, the bells began and the crossing gates lowered down as the train pulled into the station.

7. That Invincible Bunch

"Ok, now you have fun, my little bunny rabbits!" Martha sang out to the two little girls as they dutifully hung their coats up in their designated cubbies. The taller girl, her daughter Sawyer, tossed her navy blue hoodie over a hook, askew and inside out. The other girl, Vivian, took care to smooth down her wool plaid coat, with those adorable toggle buttons, before scampering off to the play kitchen area of the preschool. Little Sawyer turned and gave Martha a quick hug before following her friend.

"Love you, sweetie," Martha smiled. "Have fun."

"I love you too, Mommy!" chirped Sawyer, running to follow Vivian. Her shoelaces were untied.

"Will you also be picking up both girls today, Mrs. Zeigler?" asked the rosy-cheeked teaching assistant, who couldn't have been more than 21. She held a clipboard in her hands, checking off each child's arrival and whether they were dropped by a designated parent or helper.

"Yup, and Sally will bring them both in and out tomorrow," Martha replied. "See you after school!"

She closed the glass door to Cherry Tree Preschool behind her and proceeded down the stairs to the Park District

Building's main level. There was a faint sound of salsa music; a Zumba class was starting somewhere nearby. Those classes always looked like so much fun, except, Martha noted ruefully, if you took a Zumba class, it was sort of like admitting you were over the hill, kind of like shopping at J. Jill or Chico's. It didn't matter how beautiful the jackets looked; the brands were an instant label of middle age.

Martha was not quite there. Heck, she had a three year-old, barely out of pull-ups. By virtue of her blond hair and good genes, Martha didn't yet have any visible greys to cover up, like several of her girlfriends did. Not that her older daughter, Isla, wasn't trying her damnedest to prematurely age Martha by completely *refusing* to learn multiplication. Martha couldn't even remember learning how to multiply; it just sort of *happened* by osmosis along the way, right? Why was there such a struggle? And then there was her boy, her middle child, Mason, whose Minecraft obsession was going to drive Martha over the edge into insanity. No more with the Creepers, Ghasts and (God help us, what *are* these things?) Zombie Pig Men, please.

At least Sawyer's only fault these days was that she was a slob. But pretty much no three and a half year old was a neatnik. Except for Vivian Bundren, the little girl Martha carpooled to preschool twice a week. That girl was unnaturally fastidious; surely there was something wrong with her. Or maybe you're just being jealous, Martha reminded herself. Well, that was for sure.

Back at her minivan, Martha debated, for the eight hundredth time since last night, what she was going to do. Was there a way of getting out of this stupid mess without compromising everything? She slouched in the driver's seat with her head in her hands. There was still some time before she was going before the firing squad. Why did she want this? All she had wanted to do was meet some nice ladies and have a little social life while raising three children; was that so much to ask?

It was really all Cathy Wilson's fault. Cathy lived around the corner from Martha and her kids had all gone through

Washington. Cathy had originally suggested to Martha (what was it, three years ago?) when Isla was first starting school, that Martha might want to consider volunteering.

"When you're a Room Parent, you start getting to know all the moms in your kid's class," Cathy had said. "Since you're new to Whistler, you'll want to hook up with more gals. It will save your sanity; I've met some of my best friends that way."

Sound advice. Although Martha admittedly had had her hands amply filled with Isla beginning Kindergarten, little Mason in preschool and Sawyer barely walking, she did long for more adult duties. She had spent the past five years doing little more than watch episodes of *Caillou*, change diapers and pretend to diet. Why not get her feet wet with some grown-up stuff?

When Cathy Wilson's kids had gone to Washington, though, volunteer positions had been numerous and Committee Chairs were open for the taking to any comer. Now, you practically had to submit your credit rating to become a low-level volunteer, let alone become a Chair or get on the coveted Board. How could Martha have known that competition to be a Room Parent for a Kindergarten class would be so fierce? By not going online immediately when the email announcing sign-ups went out, Martha had missed her chance; all Kindergarten volunteer positions were filled.

"Rookie mistake," said Xander's mom, as they waited outside Washington for the morning Kindergarten class to be dismissed. "You've got to read through the emails they send home, check the dates, and jump on the sign-ups right away. You miss out on this and you're liable to miss out on taking a meaningful part in your child's experience here at Washington."

"How do you do it?" Martha was mortified. "Of course I was to be engaged with my children at school."

"You've just got to start with the basics," Xander's mom explained. "Baby steps. You can't get on the PTO board without being a Committee Chair; you can't get a Committee Chair without prior experience volunteering for the proper committees; you can't get on any of the good committees without being a Room Parent."

Martha had resigned herself to sitting on the sidelines until Isla was in First Grade, when, at the end of September, she received a surprise phone call.

"Hi there, this is Olivia Isaacson," purred the softly-inflected voice. Martha froze. Olivia was the President of Washington Elementary School's PTO, sometimes referred to (though never in her presence) as The Queen. She was the undisputed Empress of All Things related to Washington School. Originally from Charlottesville, Olivia had a BA from the College of William and Mary, an MBA from Duke's Fuqua School of Business, and a past marketing career in the Consumer Packaged Goods field. She and her husband, a hedge fund manager named Nick, had landed in the Washington school district five years ago, to the school's utter benefit.

According to the rumors, Olivia was single-handedly responsible for getting Washington school "on the map" in Whistler as one of the higher performing elementary schools in the town. She had spearheaded the effort to expand the PTO's reach, raised unheard of funds for Washington's enrichment programs, and done away with the school's practice of giving out participation trophies at the annual Science Fair, changing it to a competitive event with judges. Her daughter, Maya, was off the charts in her MAP test scores, as well as a chess champion. Olivia was renowned (and feared) for her endless capacity to organize, and create results with, Washington moms.

"Martha, your name has come up at our PTO meetings, both formally and informally. I wanted to reach out to you to gauge your interest in becoming a Room Parent"

"Oh, wow!" Martha exclaimed. "I thought I'd missed out on that. What happened?"

Olivia demurred. "You've heard about Bonnie Putnam?" Martha hadn't. "Oh? Her son Sebastian is in your daughter's Kindergarten class; I thought you would know Bonnie. Well, I will give you the short version. Bonnie Putnam's husband works in International Sales at PepsiCo, and he was recently promoted, but they want him to be located in New York. So they are moving to Connecticut as soon as possible. As a result, the morning Kindergartners need an additional parent helper. I assume you are familiar with the responsibilities of a Washington School Room Parent?"

"Oh, sure. Thanks so much for considering me; I'll be happy to help out."

"Well, we certainly appreciate your time; you'll find we are a family here. Welcome to the PTO Family."

And thus began a new chapter in Martha's life. Aside from having to spend time with Isla's surprisingly ill-tempered Kindergarten teacher, Martha loved Room Parent Duties. It was wonderful to spend time with her little girl as she learned to spell, share her ideas with others and listen to instruction. Even more wonderful was getting to know Samantha Brown and Nancy Hendricks, her co-Room Parents. Together, the organized the Halloween Party, the Holiday Party, the Valentine's Day Party, the One Hundredth Day of School Party, and the End of the Year Party, where Mrs. Grosvenor's Morning Kindergarten Class lined up and sang: "I want to be a part of it, First Grade, First Grade" to the tune of "New York New York," as proud tears rolled down Martha's cheeks.

After one year of participation, Martha was hooked. She and Nancy Hendricks in particular had completely bonded; Isla was best friends with Nancy's daughter, Annabelle, a perfect union for both the mothers and the girls. Martha continued on as a Room Parent when Isla moved on to First Grade class, jumping online the very moment the sign-ups went live. She started volunteering as well on a few of the "minor" PTO committees, like Staff Appreciation Day and Walk to School Day, to prepare herself for bigger challenges ahead. Soon enough, Mason was in Kindergarten; she had another Washington Red Bird.

The sense of truly belonging at Washington School was intoxicating. It was, for Martha, a time of email chains and luncheons, meetings, both spontaneous and scheduled through

Lois over at the school office and cleared for the Washington conference room. Martha learned to navigate and set up Sign-Up Genius. In camaraderie with other PTO Committee parents, she started calling the school's Principal Linda instead of Mrs. Wright. Martha's files at home grew and grew. She started a collection of card stock and paper plates and Elmer's glue, poster board and washable magic markers in case of a last minute need to advertise an event or assist in a classroom. She memorized Washington's tax exempt number so that her reimbursement checks would be easier to cut.

Committee work was one thing, but Martha now needed bigger and bigger fixes to keep herself going. Little gigs, like chairing Music Mayhem or Swing through the Jungle were fine, if you didn't mind your PTO career being a one-off. To prove she were truly engaged in the crusade for Whistler's children to have a meaningful education at Washington, Martha had to get aboard red-letter Committee, like the coveted Fun Run and Family Picnic, the Great Washington Spell-Off, or the Book Fair.

After a couple years at Washington, Martha had gained street cred; she exuded commitment. When some parents tried to horn their way in to volunteering at classroom events, Martha had to be adept at ensuring that the volunteer slots were distributed among the different families. A Room Parents was a gatekeeper. For example, everyone wanted to participate in Halloween and Winter (formally Christmas, then Holiday, now merely Winter) Parties; fewer people wanted Valentine's Day; only the sad leftovers got Staff Appreciation Day, which entailed separating all the flowers children brought in (reminded to do so via an email blast) and creating massive bouquets to present to the instructors, library staff, music, art and physical education teachers.

By the time Mason and Isla were in First and Third Grade, Martha was poised on the brink of greatness at Washington.

"Do you realize we still have a preschooler, Jonathon?" she asked her husband.

"Um, yeah?" he replied.

"A preschooler means we have longevity! They'll all know that I'm in for the long haul at Washington." She replied.

"Who knows this exactly?"

"Olivia and the PTO Board. I can maybe become a Chair." Martha was almost bursting with the excitement of the possibility.

"Baby, I think you need to rein it in a little bit," her husband advised. "You're starting to freak me out."

"Don't harsh my buzz, you monster; I'm having a great time!"

Nothing was more attractive to the PTO than a parent with several kids spread out over the years, thereby ensuring a lengthy tenure at Washington Elementary. Martha had stability; she was a rock-solid candidate. She had done her time as a chaperone for the kindergartners at the Nature Center when Mason was there, and for the first graders' "Opera for the Young" outing when Isla was there. PTO Committee volunteer work was exhausting, sure, but being a part of the Washington Machine meant you were a force to be reckoned with if your child ever ran into problems. Civilian parents, orphans without connection to the inner workings of the school, could be pushed around by the instructors, but PTO parents had a special dispensation.

"The teachers know what side their bread is buttered on, and you spell it P-T-O." Martha explained.

But which Committee to chair? It couldn't be just anything. You had to be somewhere that would both help your child and help you meet other moms. Sandra LaBianca had a death-grip on Book Fair, and she was pregnant again, so that was out. Book Fair would be Sandra's till the Second Coming. Martha had been prepared to settle for Hot Lunch Committee, a Sisyphean nightmare according to last year's chair, Pam Campbell ("The noise, dear God, the noise of those kids; stay far away"), until she heard there was an opening for a Co-Chair at Amazing Artists.

Amazing Artists was effectively a school-wide art showcase/competition. The Chairs coordinated with Kaylie Richards, Washington's Art teacher, and then sifted through submissions from every grade level. Martha's co-chair, Robin, was a friendly, leggy woman with a sprinkling of freckles across her nose and cheeks. Robin was a veteran PTO committee Chair who used phrases like "I'll circle back to you on that" and "we need to get the greenlight first." Her perennial perkiness was a huge asset for an event like Amazing Artists, in which some children needed to be coaxed into submitting their work.

"The hardest part," Robin said, "Is getting everything mounted on the walls straight."

Martha found the entire project delightful. She loved looking at all the riotous and squiggly, colorful and shocking artwork these growing imaginations created. It was like tending a giant, messy garden. The only rough patch was when some First Grade girls cried when their artwork did not receive special recognition. The crucial test had been passed: Martha had proven herself worthy of Co-Chairing a large-scale PTO Committee. The world was now her oyster.

Through her stellar performance as a co-chair, Martha became part of the elite Washington PTO Chair luncheons. They met once a month as a group, though many of the ladies met more frequently on an informal, purely social level. The Chair Lunches were always at a different Chair's home, always included salads and LaCroix sparkling water, and rarely disappointed. After going over business, setting up calendars and other logistics, the chatter began, usually continuing until it grew close to the end of the school day and the mothers had to disperse. This was when the girls dished the dirt on everyone else in the school. The gossip was insane.

At these luncheons, Martha learned who was getting regular Botox injections, whose kids were being tracked for the accelerated courses over at the middle school, and whose parents had threatened Mrs. Wright with a lawsuit over their child's recess skirmish. She learned whose older siblings had made it into Ivy League colleges, and whose father had once been consulted by President Obama on matters of literacy and STEM (and STEAM) projects. She learned to keep away from Tara Kirkpatrick, who seemed to think she could make the jump from Recording Secretary to being a Vice-President of PTO next year without first going through the proper pecking order of Assistant Treasurer and Future Funds.

At these luncheons, Martha learned that she needed to join the barre fitness program instead of doing hot yoga. She discovered that lowlights were more important than highlights, and that chemical peels were her newest best friend. She started growing her bangs out because you didn't want to be the one the Chairs laughingly referred to as "that mom with the 1980s hair." She bought Hunter boots with adorable liner socks and a black North Face puffer jacket. She perpetually wore running tights, as if constantly poised to hit the track. Her nails were manicured with "Nude" lacquer and filed with squared-off edges. She acquired a rainbow of scarves to accompany every outfit.

It was at a Chair Lunch that Martha found out about Liza Johannsen. According to the Chairs, Liza was "a terrible woman."

"How do you mean?" Martha asked, digging into her mixed greens with avocado.

"Well, not that this is the *real* issue," said Sandra, "But she let her son sleep in her bed till he was in Second Grade."

"She lets her daughter eat hot dogs, can you imagine? Processed meats. And peanut butter sandwiches at lunch. With all the allergies around, she's going to kill someone." Olivia was incredulous.

"Liza doesn't give a crap about anyone but herself." Sandra made a face.

"She doesn't enforce strict screen time hours either," added Olivia. "Goodness knows how that is going to affect her children's developing brains."

The bad-mouthing of Liza continued for the duration of the Chair lunch. Martha discovered that the biggest reason that Liza Johannsen was no longer in the Chairs' good graces was even darker than her insistence on peanut butter.

Last year, Liza had served as a Room Parent for her daughter Kaitlan's Third Grade class. As part of Washington School's participation in a statewide technology initiative, the Third Graders participated in an activity called "Innovation Station," wherein each student composed a brief essay on the importance of technology in the classroom. The writers of the three top essays would be invited to the State Capital on Technology Day that spring.

The Third Grade teacher, Mrs. Clarke, told Liza the names of the Innovation Station winners. As Room Parent, Liza was to send out a Washington-wide congratulatory email blast, touting the tech initiative and thanking all the children who participated. What happened next was, depending on who you talked to, either a stupid mistake or an outrageous example of racism. Liza mixed up the name of the winner, Grace Xi, with another girl in the class, her daughter's friend, Charlotte Lee. And declared the wrong student a winner. The mistake was caught immediately by Mrs. Xi, who wrote back, copying Olivia (as PTO President) and Principal Linda Wright, a scathing letter: "I'm sorry to inform you that, although White mindsets have trouble understanding it, not everyone of Asian descent is the same person. In fact, Grace and Charlotte are two entirely different little girls, with different families, different backgrounds and different personalities. We do not all look alike."

It was a mortifying, or well-deserved, comeuppance, depending who you talked to. A retraction and apology were sent out as quickly as they could be drafted. Liza was in tears, according to Cathy Wilson. So was poor little Charlotte, who thought, for a brief hour, that she was going to the special trip down to the state's capital. So was poor little Grace, who thought, for a brief hour, that she had lost the competition.

Liza did not volunteer to be a Room Parent again, nor did she attempt to become a PTO Chair. They were best served if Liza maintained a low profile, only participating in outlying committees, nothing too visible to the parents.

"Oh, God, that poor woman," Martha felt it was a bone-headed, but probably unintentional, mistake.

"Those poor girls!" murmured Sandra, spearing a wedge of blood orange with her fork. "Think of how they felt!"

"Well, of course," Martha stammered.

"Imagine how you'd feel, being the only Chinese kids in a school." Sandra pointed out.

"Isn't Charlotte's mom white?" asked Cathy.

"You ladies don't get it!" snapped Olivia. "First of all, Grace's family is from mainland China and only moved here quite recently, and Charlotte's parents were both born in the US. The point is: Liza didn't *engage* enough to look at the two girls differently. And that's not the attitude towards diversity we want to project here at Washington"

The truth was, Washington Elementary School was about 94% white. Many of the upper middle class white women who lived in Whistler felt guilty over this racial disparity, yet felt themselves helpless to change the status quo.

"Oh, of course not. It's just unfortunate, that's all." Martha said meekly.

And it was at one of the PTO Chair lunches (this one was at Sandra's house, where she served some very nice Southwestern-style chopped salad) that Martha learned about Goldilocks (code name also "G" or "Goldy" in text messages), otherwise known as Julie Calvin. Unlike her Chairs nickname, Julie was in reality small and bespectacled, with brown hair that grew almost to her waist, pulled back in a long braid. The name derived from Julie's car, a gold Cadillac Escalade.

Julie had four children (three girls and a boy) at Washington, each with a similar head of wavy brown hair. Julie's face had a cast of perpetual strain that she attempted to mask through constant shrill laughter. Goldilocks was the favorite black sheep of the PTO Chairs.

Julie had never been fully embraced by the Washington PTO social circles. She tried too hard but failed to deliver on big projects, always over-promising and under-performing, a cardinal sin with the Chairs. Pam told Martha about the time Julie had asked to assist with the Washington Fun Run and Family Picnic, a huge fall event. The PTO gave Julie the (relatively low-level) duty of procuring extra helpers for the intersections; these adult and teen volunteers were stationed at corners to both cheer on the runners and monitor traffic. Unbelievably, the day before the Fun Run, Julie claimed she'd only been able to locate three volunteers, a deficit of twelve. Working their contact list of trustworthy Washington parents, the Chairs easily filled the remaining slots on the fly, but not after mentally black-listing Julie for gross incompetence.

"Goldilocks literally cannot be trusted simply to stand on a corner and watch while runners go by," tittered Olivia, and the other Chairs laughed in chorus.

It wasn't just Julie herself, but her children, too, were suspect.

"Her oldest girl, Rachel is a menace. Did you know, she's been called to Linda's office more than ten times since the fall quarter began. I heard that her State Achievement Test scores are so low that they're dragging her class's average scores down." Sandra confided.

"The mother has checked out," said Olivia, "Simply checked out. And the daughter Rachel gets in fist fights with boys in the hallways. I've witnessed it myself. Because of children like her, Washington is going to fall behind Adams School in area rankings. We may not even get the Golden Apple again this year." Her voice was disdainful.

The Golden Apple was presented to the Whistler school that demonstrated the highest standards of excellence in academics, athletics, community outreach and social engagement. The district liked to move the Apple among the four Whistler Elementary schools, but Washington had missed out the last few years. Olivia was determined to get it back and restore respectability to their school.

Isla was now in Fourth Grade and Mason in Second. Sawyer was in her final year of Preschool at Cherry Tree. Not too long before Halloween, when the days were bright and cool but not yet too chilly, Martha brought little Sawyer to Bartleby Park on a Thursday afternoon while Mason was at soccer and Isla was at Annabelle's house for a playdate. Martha pushed Sawyer on the swings and checked out the other children and parents. A small cluster of older girls, probably Fifth Grade or so, played on the jungle gym equipment nearby.

One girl had flyaway brown hair pulled back in a loose braid; she ran around the slide, shrieking with laughter. That had to be a Goldilocks girl, Martha thought. She looks just like her mother. Two more girls appeared, looking like smaller version of the laughing child, clearly her sisters, and another girl, smaller and blond. Maya Isaacson, Queen Olivia's daughter.

"This is stupid; I'm done!" the girl yelled.

"Come on, Rachel, one more game." Maya responded. Martha had been right; the girl with the messy hair was Goldilocks' daughter. It was nice that the girls all played together, thought Martha, even though their mothers don't get along. Sometimes kids were kinder and more tolerant than adults; what lessons they can teach us.

"One last game of Monster Tag!" Maya shouted triumphantly. It really showed Olivia's superior parenting, Martha thought. Here's her daughter, Maya, inventing new games and inviting the school's scofflaw to play along with her. Refreshing. Martha pushed Sawyer gently and smiled at the other children.

Monster Tag, Martha gleaned was essentially the age-old game of tag, but instead of being "It," one child played "the Monster." If you were tagged by the monster, you became a monster yourself. Rachel Calvin was "It", and she ran around the slide and climbing wall while her sisters screamed and ran away.

"Evil monster!" Maya called, "Get away from me!" Rachel grinned, lunged at Maya and tagged her.

"Now you're a monster too!" she shrieked triumphantly.

"No, I'm not," said Maya.

"Yeah, you are," One of Rachel's sisters came to her support.

"I tagged you, Monster." Said Rachel.

Again, Maya refused to acquiesce. The Calvin girls started chanting, "Monster! Monster! Monster!"

"Ok, whatever, I have to go." And Maya ran away.

The Calvin girls continued playing Monster Tag for a few more minutes among themselves, until Julie's gold Escalade pulled into the parking lot and they all piled in. Sawyer started squirming a little, so Martha slowed the swing down and let her hop down. It was almost time to pick up Isla anyway.

That weekend, while watching Mason's Jolly Green Giants soccer team play at Bartleby Park, Martha spotted Robin Greene pacing while she spoke urgently into her cellphone. Robin waved and held up a finger to Martha, signaling her to wait a minute. After a minute or two, Robin strode over to her.

"Did you hear? Major fireworks with Goldilocks!" she whispered.

"What happened?"

"Well, I heard that Rachel, the biggest one, gathered together a gang of kids, and they were all calling poor Maya Isaacson names and chasing her."

Martha thought briefly about the game of Monster Tag she'd witnessed. "They weren't playing together? Are you sure?"

"Of course, I'm sure. Olivia called me right after it happened. I guess Maya was so upset she could barely speak."

"Because I saw Rachel Calvin playing tag with Maya at the playground just the other day. Are you sure that it's not some mistake?"

Robin stared at her. "This has to be something different. Maya was sobbing and Olivia went ballistic. She approached the mom directly, went over to her house. I guess the kid denied everything. But Olivia threatened to take legal action, so Goldilocks crumbled. She's having the kid write Maya a formal letter apologizing."

It had to be another interaction between the girls, Martha decided. There was no way you could conflate what she had seen into the story Robin just described. Besides, everyone in Washington School PTO knew that Rachel was a serial trouble-maker, whereas Maya was a model student.

Shortly thereafter, the Grand Trifecta of holidays, Halloween, Thanksgiving and Christmas, overtook Martha's (and every mother's) life for the next two months. The New Year arrived and, blessedly, her children returned back to school after winter break. PTO Board positions would be voted on coming up soon, shortly after the Great Washington Spell-Off concluded.

Every winter, Washington students prepared for the school Spelling Bee. Word lists were distributed by grade level. Kindergartners didn't participate, except within their Kindergarten classes, with very simple words and prizes for all participants. There were competitions within individual classes (Washington had two classrooms per grade level, from First through Fifth Grades), culminating in the top six students of every grade level. These finalists then went before the rest of their peers, as well as parents, in The Great Washington Spell-Off. That a Fifth Grader or occasionally an advanced Fourth Grader won every competition was rather a foregone conclusion. Nevertheless, the bee was part of Washington lore, and could always be counted on to score a write up in the local paper, along with photographs of the finalists and winner.

Martha just about burst with pride when Isla made it to her grade-level finals. She would compete, along with another Fourth Grader, in the big Spell-Off with all the teachers and all the parents present! Jonathon took off from work that day, and, for once, Martha was genuinely delighted to see her in-laws were coming as well. Isla wore her Christmas dress, which was red velvet with a dropped waist and lace collar. She even deigned to allow Martha to brush and curl her hair. Her cheeks were flushed with excitement.

"You know you're probably not gonna win, right?" asked Mason, who had no filter.

Before Martha could scold him, Isla replied, "Duh, but I made it to the Finals and I'm going up there with the smart kids!" Martha thought her heart would burst.

The Washington gymnasium was packed and humid. Latecomers were forced to stand along the walls and crowded into the doorway leading to the rest of the school. Principal Wright spoke a few words of welcome, and then the Great Spell-Off began. As expected, participants from the lower grades were knocked out fairly early. Their ten year-old was surprisingly poised, though she spoke too softly into the microphone, prompting the judges to ask her to repeat herself. Isla held on till she got stuck on "caterpillar" and then went back to her seat, shrugging her shoulders. Martha applauded madly.

"That's our Girlie," Jonathon whispered, and Martha squeezed his hand.

The final round was a showdown between Maya Isaacson and Fifth Grader Dominic Salvi. Maya put up a terrific showing, especially since she was a whole year younger than Dominic. Martha supposed that wasn't too surprising, given her mother's academic ambitions. It came down to the word "exaggerate," which Dominic spelled with only one "g." Maya spelled it correctly and subsequently won. Martha spotted Olivia beaming in the corner and gave her a thumbs-up. All the finalists had their picture taken, with Maya standing in front holding her trophy.

They piled Grandma and Grandpa Zeigler, as well as Mason and Sawyer, into their minivan after everything was over and took Isla out for a celebration dinner at the Trafalgar Café in town. Sawyer spilled ketchup all over herself and all three kids ordered giant hot fudge sundaes for dessert. Later, at home, after Jonathon's parents drove off and the kids were in bed, Jonathon poured himself and Martha a glass of scotch.

"To our little speller, Girlie!" he said, and they clinked glasses.

"Hey, lemme see your iPad. I want to relive the glory." Jonathon set it up and the two of them quietly cheered little Isla's performance at the spelling bee. Martha was especially proud of the way her Girlie flounced away, unconcerned, when she was eliminated.

"You know, caterpillar *should* be spelled with an –er at the end," she said.

"It keeps going, if you want to see the final showdown with your friend's kid," Jonathon offered.

"Why not?" Martha was in a great mood.

They watched the children who went after Isla spell, then misspell and falter, and the iMovie continued till the Spell-Off was left with only Maya and Dominic.

"See Olivia on the side there?" Martha pointed her friend out on the screen. "Look at her face; she's so nervous!"

"Can I see the iPad a second?" Jonathon asked.

"Sure, I've seen enough."

Jonathon rewound the movie and began the final showdown again. He paused the film, then watched it again.

"Um, Martha," Jonathon's voice sounded funny. "Look at this again, will you? Not the kid, the mom."

Martha perched on the arm of Jonathon's chair. The word before "exaggerate" was "separately." The quality of the digital footage on the iPad was not the highest, but Martha could plainly see Olivia mouthing the letters as Maya spoke them. Martha backed up the film and watched it again. And again.

"We're really seeing this, aren't we?" Martha asked.

"Oh, yeah," Jonathon was chuckling.

"From the angle, you can't actually see if *Maya* can see her doing it. It could be that Olivia's not even aware of what she's doing." Offered Martha.

Jonathon raised his eyebrows. "Uh huh."

Martha pulled her minivan out of the Park District Center's lot, and started back towards home and Washington School. Today was PTO Board elections day, and she was up for Recording Secretary. She'd been up much of the night, thinking about the scene she'd witnessed on the iPad: the Empress had no clothes. You had to admit, it was funny, in a sad sort of way. She couldn't wait to share the story with Cathy Wilson, the one who'd gotten her into this strange micro-world to begin with. Cathy would probably laugh for ten minutes straight; Martha smiled, visualizing her friend. She turned into Washington School's parking lot.

"Well, here goes nothing," Martha sighed. She grabbed her tote-bag, and headed for the school's Office entrance.

8. Seize the Day

Gus, their bored-looking maître-d, ushered the two families into the restaurant's back room, the one reserved for private events. Katie glanced around, dismayed; she was unsure what kind of events would be held there. A convention for hobbits, perhaps? It was a rather unfortunately narrow and claustrophobic space, with enough room behind the chairs for servers to maneuver and deliver food, but just barely. Her boyfriend's older brother, who laughed too loudly at everything, made some stupid joke about not eating too much or he'd have to go outside to burp. His mother, to her credit, glared at him. Even better, Tyler had told Katie that his (uninvited) Uncle Trevor, hearing of the get-together, had insisted he come along too. "For the booze, of course. And the ladies!" Ty had winked, but was he completely joking?

As for Katie's family: their reactions ran the gamut from her mother's awe at the sight of the Big Money soon-to-be relatives, to her father's shyness (as always, he was subdued in public situations), to her sister's unabashed scorn. Grandma came along too because, well, they couldn't just *leave* her sitting in front of the tv in her La-Z Boy till they all came home, could they? Her big brother Wally was here with Maria, who jiggled

Hannah on her lap and looked miserable. Mom had persuaded Aunt Lila to come aboard too. Because why not, at this point?

Katie wished she hadn't worn the flowered dress; it was too tight in the chest and didn't allow for deep breathing, but the sale had been too good to pass up. If she could just get through this night, she could maybe live through the next year. And after that, it would be just her and Tyler for the rest of their lives.

She had not wanted this evening to be a big deal. All Katie had desired was a nice little get-together to introduce one another before the Big Day so things wouldn't be awkward later, and they could all feel more like one big happy family. Or at least, not like total strangers. Of course, Ty had met her parents and she had met his; they had, after all, been dating throughout most of their time together in college. But now things had gone up to the next level, so to speak.

"Shit's getting real," Katie muttered, looking down at her hand. He'd gone to Tiffany's, which was frankly shocking for Tyler, who occasionally had to be reminded of delicacies like napkins and "inside voices." Already, her guy was changing for her, she realized. Or, more likely, he had asked his big brother where he should go; those two were super-close. Katie had dreamed of a Tiffany's engagement ring since she first watched Audrey Hepburn and Cat on TCM when she was home sick from school one day when she was eleven. The diamond was a whole carat, round cut, and in the trademarked Tiffany setting. The band was rose gold; her friend Emma had said that rose gold was just a fad, but Emma was an idiot. The ring was perfect.

Louisa surveyed the room, raising her eyebrows. Katie had made a fuss about how she wanted this little party of hers to be local. Of course, she really meant local for her. Meaning Katie could stay where she was in the city while all the rest of her family had to schlepp in from Michigan City to get there. Why couldn't she just have sucked it up and gone back home for the weekend? Was it because Katie didn't think there was enough to impress her new family in northwest Indiana?

Precious Katie couldn't be bothered to move her petite little butt for anyone now that she was Getting Married.

You could see that Katie was changing already, Louisa thought. Katie never used to give a crap about talking to any relatives or adults, other than their parents, but look: there she was, chatting it up with Aunt Lila and Grandma Wojcik, the same Grandma Wojcik who house Katie used to hate to visit. Joke's on us, Louisa sighed; now Granny's living in our house.

Katie and her boyfriend (excuse me, fiancé) had picked out the venue for the engagement dinner. Clearly, they had done so without looking at the party room, but that was beside the point. The place was near Tyler's condo, and was appropriately named *Carpe Diem*. Her mother had gushed about how "sweet" and "perfect" the name was for the young couple, while Katie and Tyler *beamed*. Katie did a lot of *beaming* these days. At least the place wasn't one of those glassy shiny hipster joints that Louisa detested. In fact, Louisa admired the dark wood and cozy feel of the place; she might have enjoyed *Carpe Diem* had she not been there for the purpose of getting the Wojcik family together with all the Carmody family. Or rather, having the Polish serfs from provincial Indiana all drive in like the Joads to meet the filthy rich dining hall Jay Gatsby types. It was pure cliché: elite suburban mice meet blue collar mice. Louisa could practically write an English paper on it already.

Not that her mother, Renata, appeared to notice anything screwy about this evening. On the contrary, she was in fine form, talking loudly, gesticulating wildly with her hands, laughing too hard at jokes and wanting to kiss everyone. Had she been nipping Dubonnet prior to their leaving home to bolster her courage?

Renata had tried too hard when picking out her wardrobe that evening. She had shot for elegant, but only made it as far as tacky. Louisa had advised her mother not to wear the dress with the cut-outs on the shoulders.

"It's called the 'cold-shoulder' look, honey," Renata had said. "Everybody is wearing it."

"Yeah," Louisa had muttered in response, low enough so that Renata couldn't hear her, "Two or three years ago." It was too cliché to be embarrassed of one's mother, Louisa knew, but she really couldn't help herself. And Renata, bless her heart, made it easy. She meant well, Louisa guessed, but she could tell that Renata was completely starry-eyed at the prospect of the new in-laws. Louisa may as well have been a potted plant since the day Katie showed off her vulgar, ostentatious diamond ring ("Did I tell you? It's from Tiffany's!") to their parents.

The lines had been drawn since the girls were practically babies. Louisa was the smart one; Katie was the pretty one. Katie had boyfriends and secret admirers and a crew of girls who had followed her around like a string of baby ducklings ever since the Third Grade. Katie was Little Mary Sunshine. Teacher's Pet. Perfection. Louisa, on the other hand, was the also-ran, named after one of the Von Trapp kids, the one that no one remembers. The only names from *The Sound of Music* that people remember are Liesl and Gretl -- maybe Brigitta on a good day, but certainly not Louisa. To make matters worse, Louisa couldn't even sing.

But the Smart/Pretty dichotomy didn't really work, Louisa grumbled to herself, because Katie was actually the smarter one. Maybe Louisa could be called the More Cynical sister? Although she certainly read more books than Katie (admittedly, not terribly difficult to achieve; Katie was not a huge reader, while Louisa was a voracious one), Louisa lagged behind her sister grade-wise.

Louisa's relationship with Katie could be summarized in one anecdote: back in middle school, Louisa had once received an anonymous Valentine's Day card in her locker that read:

"Roses are red,

Violets are blue.

Your sister is beautiful:

So what happened to you?"

Her mother had, of course, insisted that the card had been some boy's misguided effort at flirtation, but any fool could see that it was a girl's handwriting. At that point in her life, at twelve, Louisa renounced her adolescent Quest for Beauty; she was going to live a life *of* books and *for* books. Let Katie live in her princess castle and be adored. That was not how Louisa the Von Trapp Girl Wojcik was going to live her life. Renata repeatedly, and not very charitably, pointed out to Louisa that if she paid more attention to her appearance, she could be a knock-out.

"Really?" Louisa would respond dryly, peering over her glasses. "A knock-out? I must be mistaken; I thought we were in the 21st Century now, not Victorian England. If someone is interested in me for how I look, then they are obviously just superficial."

"Aw, honey, I say that when I gain a couple extra pounds, too," Renata chimed in.

It was not the least surprising to anyone in the Wojcik family that Katie got engaged right after graduating from college. That her fiancé was the scion of Old Money, however, took everyone aback. Sure, the two had dated in college for a few years, but frankly, no one expected the romance to progress past the fraternity parties and into the realm of the real world. Tyler was nice and kind of cute, which sort of complicated the whole deal in Louisa's mind. Had he been a creep, Louisa could have dismissed the whole lame wedding as bullshit. But there he was, a nice guy, engaged to her sister.

"You get to be my Maid of Honor!" Katie had chirped, which meant that Louisa had to hold a bridal shower for Katie at some point, and take charge of the Bridesmaids Luncheon, not to mention the dreaded bachelorette party. Louisa was not the party planning type.

"Isn't that why you joined a sorority?" Louisa had responded. "I thought bridesmaids came along with the pledge pins."

As it turned out, Katie planned on having no fewer than six bridesmaids, in addition to Louisa as the Maid of Honor. She was also planning on having little Hannah, their brother Wally's daughter, as a Flower Girl. Can you just imagine seeing tiny little Hannah going down the aisle with a basket of rose petals? It was too adorable, Katie had exclaimed. She hadn't finalized anything yet, but Katie confided to Louisa that she wanted her color scheme to be black and white. Katie, the bride, in white, and literally everyone else in black.

"So that everyone can tell which one is the bride, right?" Louisa inquired.

"I want it to be elegant." Katie said. "And don't worry, black is very slimming." She glanced at her sister.

Rather than letting everybody sit where they wanted to, Katie and Tyler created little place-cards. Carmodys and Wojciks were carefully sprinkled among each other. Grandma Wojcik squinted at a card, then pronounced she couldn't see a thing, and sat down at the head of the table, despite Katie's efforts to move her. On Tyler's side, special care had been taken to ensure that (the heretofore uninvited) Uncle Trevor's seat was *not* integrated; he was surrounded by Carmodys, ostensibly to keep him from doing or saying anything untoward.

Ty told Katie, "Trust me, it's better for everyone this way." As if sensing he had been intentionally corralled away, Uncle Trevor called loudly to the waiter to bring another bottle of Chianti.

Dinner would be served, Tyler announced, family style. Baskets of warm bread were distributed, along with butter pats nestled in bowls of ice-cubes. Salads and cups of minestrone would be passed out shortly. Entrees were Chicken Vesuvio, Linguini Frutta di Mare, and Four Cheese Tortellini. Bottles of Chianti were distributed throughout the table. You could hear Rosemary Clooney singing "Mambo Italiano" over the stereo. Voices rose, along with the guest's spirits. It was a charming scene.

Renata Wojcik lovingly gazed around the table at her children: Wally the family man, Katie the bride-to-be, and Louisa the intellectual. Thank God she had gone ahead with that knee surgery last year instead of putting if off any longer; she wouldn't want to be limping down the aisle on the big day. Peter had told her to quit delaying, and it turned out he was right. Now the second of her babies was settling down. She was a lucky mama.

Louisa was still so young; Renata didn't have to start worrying about her settling down just yet. Renata could wait a bit longer for Louisa to find herself a guy. But, really, why couldn't her daughter smile a little more? Speaking of smiling, who would've figured that her mother-in-law would still be around to enjoy this? Peter's mother, Matilda, moved in with Renata and Peter about five years ago. Her husband Stanley was long gone, and Tillie sometimes had trouble getting out of bed and up off the toilet.

Renata turned to her mother-in-law, wizened and frail, but resplendent in her "fancy" slate blue dress with the pewter buttons down the front. Her thin white hair was twisted into a tidy bun on the top of her head. Renata shouted, "How you doing, Mom? You have enough to eat?"

Tillie nodded. "This marinara sauce is almost as good as mine. Not quite, but close." Uncle Trevor Carmody, whose broad frame dwarfed Tillie, looked down at the tiny woman putting away huge forkfuls of linguini and laughed in agreement.

"Now this is one smart lady! We need to dance together when these kids get hitched."

Tillie shrugged and nodded. "If I'm not dead before then." Trevor had to cover his mouth with his napkin so that he didn't spray the table with his guffaws.

"You need to watch that," Tillie warned him. "Or they'll have to give you the Heimlich maneuver. That's how my Stanley went. He choked on a fishbone. Nobody knew about the Heimlich maneuver then, so we all just sat there and watched him choke."

Uncle Trevor, not quite sure if Tillie was pulling his leg or not, took a long drink from his water glass.

Tyler's older brother, William, was already drunk. He made several toasts to the happiness of his baby brother, and welcomed the Wojciks into the family. Louisa noticed that he leered at Katie, which was disgusting, though not surprising. Katie did look extra pretty tonight, in that *precious* little Kate Spade "fit and flare" dress with the pastel floral print. Just as perky as a little bunny rabbit. Dad was shedding some of his usual social awkwardness, thank goodness.

"So, have you kids set the date yet?" asked Mrs. Carmody.

Katie smiled prettily, of course. "We'd like to have the wedding next year. At my parish here in the city." Louisa knew for a fact that Katie did not belong to any Catholic church in the city, and was in the process of shopping around for one. But she smiled with those pearly whites and of course nobody said boo to her.

Renata's face fell, "You mean you're not going to have the wedding back home? I thought you'd want to have the wedding at Saint Stanislaus Kostka's and the reception over at Whittaker Woods."

"We did discuss that, Mrs. Wojcik," Ty interjected, "but with Katie living and working in the city, I didn't want her to have to travel to plan everything. We'll have a city wedding so both families will have to drive a bit to get to it. But don't worry, it'll be a great celebration!"

Tyler to the rescue. Katie beamed again. The couple had already announced that they would be paying for much of the wedding themselves, without needing much from Katie's parents. Tyler had a Trust Fund and a job at Dean Witter. No more really need be said, Louisa surmised. Her wedding would be a pain in the butt for everyone except her. What a shocker.

"As long as you go before God to pledge yourselves, that's what's important," Peter pronounced solemnly. He was beginning to get slightly in his cups, Renata noticed, and his eyes sparkled a bit. Pete always got sentimental when it came to his girls.

Hal appeared touched by Peter's words. "Aw, Pete, we'll make sure the kids do it right, won't we? Tyler's a lucky, lucky guy to find a wife as wonderful as Katie. He could not have done

105

any better!" The table generally applauded. Tyler gently held Katie's hand, while Will elbowed his brother in the ribs and laughed.

Great Aunt Lila, Grandma Tillie's sister, sat next to Joyce. She cleaned her plate of tortellini and asked, "So what kind of name is Carmody?"

Joyce paused, "Um, I believe it's Gaelic, Irish. Isn't that right, Hal?" Hal nodded. "I'm not Irish at all, though. My maiden name was Sitek."

Lila fairly shrieked with delight. "*Czy ty jestes Polakiem?*" Joyce smiled.

"Yes, but I can't speak any--"

Lila cut her off, "Tillie! *Ona est Polka!*" And once again, the table applauded. Uncle Trevor whooped.

"I think this calls for another toast!" he shouted.

"Oh, hey now, Mike--" Joyce began.

"*Na zdorovie!*" cried Tillie, which Trevor echoed.

Will gestured to their server to bring out a couple more bottles of Chianti. After all, this was his kid brother. Peter and Hal discovered that they both loved old movie musicals, so Peter quizzed Hal on the extent of his knowledge.

"Ok, but can you tell me what was the name of the gal who sang for Deborah Kerr in *The King and I?*" he asked.

"The one whose voice they dubbed in? Oh, crap, it's on the tip of my tongue. Same one who sang for Natalie Wood in *West Side Story*, wasn't it?" Hal pursed his lips as he thought of the answer.

"Give up?" Peter asked. "Marnie Nixon."

"Yes, that's right! Marnie Nixon!" Hal bellowed, and the two men laughed together.

The new bottles of wine were emptied. Louisa bowed her head, looking down at her phone. She had been sending her friend, Dina, comical text messages, commenting on the events of the evening. Dina wanted a photo or two, so Louisa surreptitiously took a couple shots of Uncle Trevor with his arm around Grandma Tillie. Louisa added a caption for extra impact: "LOL Grandma's being a cougar tonight with Tyler's uncle!"

Will got up from his seat a little shakily and stumbled out the door to the restroom. Joyce, Renata and Lila chatted together gaily, gesturing with their hands as they spoke. Tyler whispered something in Katie's ear that made her smile and flap at him with her hand in mock anger.

Will came back into the party room, singing along with the stereo in a very passable baritone. "Like-a you, like-a me, back in old Napoli, that's amore!" Aunt Lila and Renata clapped their hands.

Hannah, who had fallen asleep in Maria's lap, woke up and began to cry, so Maria jiggled her until she quieted down.

9. Coffee Spoons

The Whitesides lived just off the corner of Sixth and Chester in a modest, mustard-colored ranch house. Black-eyed Susans lined the path to the front door, and a rusty basketball hoop stood next to the driveway. The burning bush in the front yard had been pruned to a neat circle.

Sunlight reflected off the large picture window in front. If you looked more closely, you might detect smudges on the lower edge of the glass panes, about eighteen inches above the floor. These were snout marks; the Whitesides were a dog household. But not just any dog: the inimitable Roscoe, also known as Stubby McNuggets, also known as You Old Hound Dog, and various other endearments.

Oliver Whiteside had researched dogs for weeks, once Paige and Glenn finally acquiesced and said they would allow him to get a puppy. At first, Ollie wanted to rescue a dog from the local shelter, certainly a noble idea. The family had made several trips to the Whistler Humane Society and the nearby Midwest Animal Rescue, falling in love with each new pup he saw. Until, that is, the boy saw a photo of a Basset Hound online; then it was all over. Ollie could not possibly have any pet other than a mournful, bow-legged floppy-eared hound dog. They got him from a breeder downstate, and Oliver named his new friend Roscoe.

You would never know how old this dog is from how crazy-impatient he gets to take his morning walks, Paige thought, as she clipped the harness behind Roscoe's broad back and attached the leash. Already, the squat basset hound was whimpering and pulling Paige to the door. Roscoe had never been particularly obedient, and was especially not so in his old age. He still nibbled at Paige's knees if she wasn't fast enough with the leash.

"Oh, come on, you," she admonished. "I haven't tied my shoes yet. Hold your damn horses."

At almost ten years old now, Roscoe carried himself with the comical dignity of all basset hounds, and the venerability his age merited. He was a tri-colored basset, mostly white, but with brown ears and head, and black spots on his back and sides. Ever mournful-appearing, Roscoe nevertheless skipped with stubby-legged happiness when the temperature dipped below fifty degrees. Paige finished lacing her sneakers, groaning as she stood up.

"Did you hear that?" she asked Roscoe. "My joints are creaking." Her remarks were met with an impatient sneeze, followed by a yawn.

"Alright, buddy, here we go." Paige zipped her ancient taupe barn jacket up all the way to her throat and put on a pair of tortoiseshell sunglasses. Before stepping out, she plugged her cellphone into the charger on the counter. Paige liked absolute solitude on her walks, just her and the dog. And really, nothings was going to happen during the forty-five minutes or so that Paige and Roscoe were out together. Whatever happened, she would get back to whoever later. There was nobody that was going to bother her now.

It was a bright morning, and Paige's progressive contact lenses, begrudgingly purchased after years of fumbling with readers, made her eyes hyper-sensitive to bright light. The shades also made Paige feel like she was travelling incognito. Though, really, who else would be walking the only basset hound in Whistler? This was a village of hypoallergenic labradoodles and golden doodles, not lugubrious, strong-smelling hounds like Roscoe, who was as stubborn as he was sweet-natured.

Roscoe hopped clumsily down the porch steps, then buried his snout in the bushes separating the Whiteside's home from the Burke's next door. As always, when out with Roscoe, Paige mused ruefully how *other* dogs walked with their owners, maintaining a brisk pace and providing a morning constitutional for both pet and human. Roscoe's gait, on the other hand, vacillated between a waddle and a dead stop, while he investigated various scents. It was sort of a game he played with Paige: how long would she allow him to snuffle in the underbrush before tugging on his leash and saying, "Come on, you."

They turned onto Chester and started walking north, towards the school and the park beyond. Dutifully, Roscoe lifted a leg at favorite landmarks: the sign marking the intersection of Sixth and Chester; the low stone wall in front of Jan Chou's house; the maple tree in front of the house whose family Paige didn't know, but thought of as "the people with the pissy dachshund." Said dachshund predictably let out manic yaps from behind the chain-link fence as Roscoe placidly urinated on the maple tree.

They passed Mark and Colleen Tomasso's place, notable for the ceramic duck that squatted near the front door. Because it was November, Colleen's duck wore a jaunty checkered coat and hunting cap (soon it would sport a Santa coat and hat). As usual, Roscoe eyed the duck warily, turning back to give it a final "ruh" of defiance as he and Paige passed.

Once they were beyond the Tomasso's house, the basset hound sped up. Roscoe whimpered and pulled Paige forward as they neared a brick bungalow with a wide porch. Terra cotta urns filled with golden chrysanthemums stood at either side of the entryway, and wind chimes gonged softly. A slender man with steel grey hair was busy using a squeegee on the windows from atop a short stepladder. He turned when he heard Roscoe's whining.

"Oh, there's my boy!" the man grinned, and started down the ladder. Roscoe, losing all his hound-ish dignity, flopped on his side and exposed his pale, spotted belly for a rub.

"Oh, yes, that's a good boy, Roscoe!" the man said. "Such a good boy."

"He gets no love at home, you know," Paige deadpanned. "None at all."

"Oh, I can tell; poor boy has to search the neighborhood for a belly rub, doesn't he?" Roscoe's eyes rolled back in delight and his fat, round forepaws waved in the air.

"Hey, buddy, would you like a treat?" And like lightning, Roscoe was back on his feet, following the man to his garage. "I think I might just have something back here for you."

"You really don't have to," Paige began.

"Aw, what else am I going to do with these things? It's not like we have a dog here." The man responded. "I just keep treats for the special boys, the really *good* boys, right Roscoe?"

"Thanks again," called Paige as Roscoe munched his treat. "Have a good one."

Paige rarely deviated from her current route, up Chester Street past Washington Elementary School to Bartleby Park down around the Bowl and then looping back home again. They had walked this route together since Roscoe was a fifteen pound puppy who kept stepping on his own improbably long ears; now Roscoe weighed in at a lumbering seventy pounds of solemnity. Only rain showers (for a hound, Roscoe was surprisingly delicate about getting raindrops on his back) or blustery, sub-zero wind chills stopped Paige from her eight block loop.

This morning was particularly glorious, autumn in full splendor. The air was chill. Russet and gold leaves formed a lattice-tracing against the sky. Roscoe skipped and snuffed past Washington Elementary, behind the playground, past the parking lot and onto the park. That school held years of memories for Paige, almost all of them cherished. Her boy had gone there once upon a time.

Paige recalled with absolute clarity dropping Oliver off at Washington for his first day of Kindergarten a million years ago. He had worn that dark green tee shirt with the picture of the rocket on it, Paige remembered. As usual during Oliver's younger years of boyhood, he had needed a haircut, and his dark blonde curls had tumbled in his eyes. If not for all the photos memorializing that auspicious first day, Paige doubted she'd have remembered the specific shirt. When was it – thirteen, fourteen or fifteen years ago? She certainly recalled the struggle to get the boy moving. Ollie could never get himself out of bed in the morning even as a five year-old. Thank goodness for afternoon Kindergarten, heaven-sent for the mothers of late sleepers.

That time had moved so insanely quickly – those years from Kindergarten through Fifth Grade at Washington. And then Oliver was off to Whistler Middle School, a tenure which required him to catch the bus at the corner of Sixth Street every morning. Those days, Oliver was frequently late, even with little Ted Monarch, his best buddy, coming to the door and bellowing up the Whitehouse's stairs: "You're gonna miss the bus, bro!" Finally, Oliver himself, hair in corkscrews, pillow wrinkles on his cheek, would fumble down the stairs and out the door. Those were the days when Ol had moved from being a pink-cheeked little cherub to a strange, lanky stick creature, all elbows and knees and awkwardness. His friend Ted grew so much that Oliver nicknamed him "Too Tall Ted."

They had gotten Roscoe from the breeder downstate around the time Oliver started middle school. Glenn thought that eleven years old was a good age for a boy to get his first dog; he'd be old enough to take care of his pet responsibly, and large enough so that, as the dog, grew, Ollie would be sturdy enough to walk him.

For boy and dog, it had been love at first sight. Oliver played and rolled on the floor with Roscoe; the dog chased his boy around the house, barking his surprisingly deep "ruh, ruh!" Oliver called Roscoe "Brother Hound" and would blow on his snout till Roscoe licked him on the lips. His track pants and tee shirts would be covered with Roscoe's short brown and white hairs.

When Oliver left for school in the mornings, both in middle school and throughout high school, Roscoe would howl mournfully as he watched his boy walk away down the driveway. The dog's ghastly howls then continued for a good ten minutes afterwards. Paige was so amused by Roscoe's exercise that she videotaped it and texted a clip to Oliver as he rode the bus.

"Poor dumb hound," Ollie texted back. "Doesn't he know I'll be back soon?"

Paige reached the grassy bowl at the center of Bartleby Park. A few years ago, before Bonnie Putnam and her family had moved to the East Coast, Paige had taken Roscoe here every morning to run around with little Duncan, Bonnie's mutt. Of course, "mutt" was not how Bonnie referred to Duncan; she called him a miniature cava-poo, which, in Paige's opinion, was just another name for a mutt. That dog had been crazy, running around like a black and white mop with fluffy feet that looked like something out of a Dr. Suess book. After all the little ones filed into Washington Elementary School, Bonnie and Paige would let their dogs off-leash to romp and snuffle and bark together.

How Roscoe had loved the Putnam's pooch. He used to pull Paige all eight blocks to Bartleby when Duncan had been around. After the Putnams moved, poor Roscoe would sniff around the Bartleby Park, searching for his former pal. Bonnie and Paige had emailed each other about perhaps bringing the dogs to visit with each other when the Whitesides went out to Cape Cod in the summer, but they never got around to doing it. As much as she loved the dog, Paige did not relish the idea of driving across country with him, or putting him in the cargo hold of an airplane while they flew off to Providence.

Paige thought it might be nice to write to Bonnie and see what she and Gene and the kids were up to these days. Bonnie's children were a bit younger than Oliver. They would be close to high school by now, though, if not already starting. Bonnie probably had a million things on her mind these days. High school was tough. You think that middle school is tough, and then high school and dating and standardized tests and sports teams and social status come into play. And it was likely to be even harder on girls these days, who all seemed forced to grow up so much more quickly. Bonnie had both a boy and girl, only thirteen months apart in age. Hope Bonnie makes it through the kids' puberty without too much hassle, Paige thought with a smile.

They reached the center of the Bowl, the part of Bartleby Park that the Village of Whistler flooded in the winter for ice skating and hockey. Ollie and his buddy Ted had skated a bit together over the years, but their true love was basketball. Oliver had been a decent player, good enough to make Whistler's high school team as point guard, though not as a starter. Too Tall Ted, of course, had been a starter, and a bit of a star his junior and senior years, on the high school team. Ted had even managed to get noticed by a few colleges in the area --- no big national programs like at the university downstate, but good enough to offer the young man some impressive scholarships as an incentive to enroll.

Jason Monarch, Ted's good-natured father, had even floated the possibility that, with the money he'd save them, Ted might be getting his own car (used, of course, nothing fancy) for graduation. It was a bone of contention with Ted, who had a younger sister and brother in need of constant carpooling, that he rarely had personal access to the family car.

It is a truth universally acknowledged, thought Paige, that a teenage boy in possession of a driver's license will badger his parents for use of the car. As an only child in a two-car family, Oliver wasted no opportunity to importune, sweet-talk or cajole Paige into letting him drive. She didn't much like letting him, other than across town to her mother's to do errands, or to pick up a pizza at Slice o' Heaven. But Glenn said it was a guy thing, that he had been the same way at Oliver's age.

"Freedom, hon." He had stated many times. "We menfolk like our freedom."

That night, Paige had been intently watching CNN, so Oliver had asked Glenn if he minded him taking the car on a McDonald's run.

"Isn't getting kind of late?" Glenn had asked.

"Growing teen, much hunger. Need greasy burgers stat!" Oliver replied.

"Don't scratch the paint then, mate." Glenn had said, with a bad fake British accent.

"Awroight then, mate," And Ollie was out the door and into the car.

Paige hadn't looked up from Anderson Cooper.

Coming down the edge of the bowl was a stiff-legged Golden Retriever wearing a blue bandana around his neck. Paige waved at the dog's human, Karen Falco, a stocky woman in her sixties, looking as jaunty as her dog in a bright red fleece jacket and a baseball cap with the legend "Whistler Little Theatre" stitched on it. Roughly simultaneously, the two women crouched down and unclipped both dogs from their leashes. Roscoe loped away to roll with the Golden, his tongue lolling rapturously. The Golden placed his snout down on his forepaws, rump in the air, in the universal posture of "play with me!"

"Old Goose is looking a lot perkier today," Paige commented.

"Well, you know, I think he's been trying extra hard to keep me busy now that Don is gone. He's been doing all sorts of kooky things, haven't you, baby? When was it, maybe two nights ago, Goose woke me up in the middle of the night and I was like 'Oh, m'gosh, what is it now?' I thought that maybe he had that bad poop thing going again, but it ended up being nothing. But before then, he was limping. I think maybe it was that poodle – we saw Steve Tromley with that crazy Gertie – and you know how aggressive that one can be."

Paige nodded.

"So, Goosie's happy to see his special buddy, Roscoe, aren't you, sweetie? Do you want a treat, Roscoe? Of course he does! Look at those eyes; couldn't you just die? They are so expressive. And those sweet, sweet ears. I could just eat you up, baby!"

The two women didn't talk much to each other, but kept their conversation centered on the antics of their two dogs, laughing when they looked especially silly, or reprimanding them if they played a little too rough.

Goose and Roscoe frolicked together for a few more minutes, until Karen spotted a couple walking around the rim of the Bowl. She whistled for Goose, who dutifully trotted back to her, allowing Karen to re-clip his leash. Unlike his obedient companion, Roscoe cheerfully loped towards the couple with Paige chased after him.

"Hey," she yelled. "Roscoe, get back here!"

A Village of Whistler Ordinance dictated that all dogs must be on leash in any public park or public space. Of course, people constantly violated that rule, and the local police turned a blind eye if nobody minded. If any citizens were to report the unleashed dogs, however, the cops would be obligated to put an end to canine playtime. Discretion was the better part of valor. Paige was winded by the time she finally caught up with Roscoe, and clipped his leash back on, swearing under her breath. She was not in the mood to have a pair of spooked, huffy animal-haters angry at her.

To Paige's relief, the couple seemed more amused than frightened by the sight of Roscoe's flapping jowls and billowing ears as he approached them. That *was* one good thing about a basset hound, Paige thought. No one is going to be terrified when one of these chubby little gators rolls up to them.

"Sorry about that," she called to the couple, raising a hand. They smiled back.

Since Paige was already a good fifty yards away from Karen and Goose, she simply turned and waved goodbye. It was getting late; Roscoe would be looking forward to his nap. Paige hadn't thought about dinner yet. Probably Glenn would be getting back too late again anyway. She might heat up some of that leftover pea soup. Or maybe just throw together something with chicken. They climbed back up the edge of the bowl, past the parking lot and Washington Elementary, and started back down Chester Street towards home. A bit irritably, Paige tugged on Roscoe's leash to hurry him up.

When Oliver hadn't come back from McDonalds within an hour, Paige finally looked up from CNN. She texted her son peevishly, asking if he intended on returning home that evening. When Ollie didn't respond, her texts increased in urgency. "It's a school night, hot shot." "Hey, kiddo, are you going to answer me?" "Call me. Now." She called him, but Oliver's phone went straight to voicemail. Paige told herself that the feeling in the pit of her stomach was irrational. Of course it was; there was no reason to think otherwise, Glenn told her. Oliver was always very trustworthy; he wouldn't just dash off to meet a girl or see a movie without telling them.

Not long afterward, there was a knock on the door. Glenn answered it because Paige couldn't move. A police officer walked into their family room and asked if they were the parents of Oliver F. Whiteside of this address. He told them there had been an accident.

There was no human space large enough to contain her pain and guilt. It was palpable, and covered Paige in a silent scream. Time stopped.

The town embraced Ollie's tragedy as its own; overnight, his story became part of Whistler's mythology. Blue ribbons were wrapped around all the trees on Chester Street, just like they had done that time when Pat Kauffman's little girl on the other side of town had died from a brain tumor. Clusters of weeping high school girls carried cellophane-bound bouquets to the sharp curve on Route 40 where Ollie's car had hit the guardrail at just the wrong angle going just a little too fast and flipped.

Chief Helder of the Whistler Police wrote a solemn Letter to the Editor of the Whistler Chronicle, using the opportunity to emphasize not only the community's shared sadness, but the need for young people especially to avoid their phones while driving. It appeared that Oliver was distracted at the time of the accident. Most likely, they concluded, he had been texting a friend.

With that discovery, Ollie's accident stopped being something terrible that happened to her boy, and became, instead, a Cause. "#putdownyourphone" started trending locally. Students held rallies and took pledges to keep away from their devices while driving. Camera crews from the television stations in the city filmed the candlelight vigil that the Whistler High Senior Class had organized. Newscasters from the city led off segments with: "In this close-knit small suburb, a young man's texting death prompts community action, bringing people together in sadness." It was obscene.

Paige could not attend the vigils or read the heartfelt but helplessly maudlin notes that were left at her front door, along with cheap plush teddy bears. Glenn quietly arranged for the gifts and flowers to be donated to local hospitals. He spoke also to the crowds of well-wishing friends and neighbors, who had no idea what to do or say, but just wanted to let him know they were there. He thanked everyone individually, while Paige lay curled up on their bed upstairs.

Time moved grotesquely slowly. Sleeping was impossible, so Paige took Valium, which gave her dry mouth and made her dizzy, but she did at last close her eyes. Nothing became bearable; nothing eased. One day was worse than the next, if that was even possible.

And then there was Paige's mother, Fran. Frances Pavlik lived just outside Whistler, and had spent the last eighteen years adoring her handsome "O-Boy." Paige's brother Rick, along with Margo and the kids, had moved to Houston when Rick's girls were babies, so Ollie had been the only grandchild Fran had seen on a regular, almost daily, basis. Even by doting grandmother standards, Fran adored Oliver to distraction, and saw him as often as she could manage.

In recent years, since getting his driver's license and with the growing decline of Fran's eyesight, Oliver would drive Fran to the grocery store. To Paige, the boy would roll his eyes and sigh, but Paige insisted. "It's such a little thing, and it makes Grandma so happy. She's not always going to be around for us, you know." And Oliver would go. Of course he would; he loved any opportunity to drive that car.

Fran's reaction to the accident at least allowed Paige to focus on something outside herself. Her mother looked like a bad cartoonist's illustration of Grief. For Oliver's Visitation, Fran had attempted to look presentable and had applied make-up to a face completely battered by weeping. She had slashes of black eye-liner already smearing with fresh tears, and crimson circles of blusher on her cheeks. She was so comically tragic that Paige's cocoon of self-hatred melted. She put her arm around Fran's trembling, narrow shoulders and sat her mother down with a glass of water, while Glenn, his own eyes swollen to silver slits, shook hands and whispered "Thank You" to the endless line of mourners snaking through Rothman Funeral Home. Paige was not even very much surprised, when nine days after the funeral, Fran suffered a stroke as she dressed for church choir practice. Paige was frankly jealous that her mother had been able to escape life now that Oliver was dead, while she hadn't.

This second family death elevated the Whiteside tragedy to legendary status in Whistler, the stuff of homilies for miles around.

"If one more person sends me a card about how Grandma Fran wanted to join her Ollie boy in heaven, I'm going to--"

"You're going to what, Paige?" Glenn asked. "Jesus, they're just trying to help."

"I don't want any fucking help." And Paige had stomped away, leaving Glenn alone again. He was alone a lot.

Glenn drank glass after glass of Knob Creek, but didn't get drunk. He and Paige passed each other like ghosts, occasionally nodding in acknowledgement of the other, but incapable of talking. He buried himself in his work, staying late and leaving early. Instead of coming to bed, he went watched tv in the basement or spent hours on his laptop. Sometimes Glenn went out with colleagues from work, who felt he needed to get out more and enjoy himself. Paige didn't care; she wanted to be alone anyway.

It took Roscoe three months to stop waiting for Oliver to come home. He refused to budge from his familiar position in front of the picture window, where he sat and howled. He wants his Brother Hound, Paige thought hysterically. When Roscoe finally abandoned his lookout post, Paige felt betrayed, yet relieved. Time barely moved, which was awful. But then again, when time went on, it went on without Oliver, which was worse.

You don't get over anything, you don't ever move on after your child dies, Paige thought. When you live through the days after, it's not that you're being strong; you're just being not dead. So, hurray for me; I'm not-dead. And I'll be not-dead every day now till I die. She sat on Ollie's bed; she could still almost smell his hair on his pillow. She couldn't bear the thought of packing up his things, but nor could she bear the thought of seeing them day after day, without her son.

It was Too Tall Ted Monarch who first came up with the idea of organizing a three-on-three basketball memorial tournament in honor of Oliver last year. Along with several of Ollie's old buddies from the Whistler basketball team, Ted created the "Ollie Hoops," tourney and arranged for it to be played at the new Park District Center that was going up. All the proceeds from registration went to local charities. Paige could not bring herself to go to the tournament, but laid in bed watching episodes of *Top Chef* and drinking Sauvignon Blanc till she had to kneel over the toilet and vomit up her self-loathing. It was Glenn who got up next to Ted, and with a tremulous voice, thanked the participants for honoring Oliver's memory.

Time somehow went on without her boy. The infants down the street became toddlers, the seasons changed, sometimes it was sunny, sometimes it snowed, and Paige walked the dog. Oliver's nineteenth birthday passed, and although Paige spent much of the day in a fetal position in her closet, rocking with the force of her sobs, she woke up the next morning not-dead. And the morning after that as well.

She never quite stopped hating everyone else's children for getting to grow up. She never stopped hating herself for not looking up that night and saying goodbye. She never stopped hating Glenn for being so much better at faking it through life than she could. Time crawled by.

Sometimes now, Paige rubbed Glenn's back as she passed his chair in the den, and Glenn would pat the back of Paige's hand, but they didn't speak much. There was nothing to say anymore. No longer needing Ollie's college fund, they had more than enough money to travel and do all those things that empty-nesters were supposed to long to do, but of course, they didn't. Glenn's hair was peppered silver overnight it seemed. Paige had trouble focusing her vision, and went to the optometrist. She got progressive lenses. Minutes passed

This year, at the second annual "Ollie-Hoops Three-On-Three Tourney", Paige made it out of the bedroom and over to the Park District Center. She had managed to stand and smile at the podium, even deigning to wear a tournament t-shirt. Ted was now a sophomore in college somewhere, looking like a grown man these days. He didn't look nearly as scrawny as he used to look when he and Oliver played around together. To Paige's bemusement, Too Tall Ted was now a handsome young man. Paige started to hate him for that, but she was getting tired of hating everyone and everything all the time.

She stood next to Glenn as Ted gave his opening remarks for Ollie Hoops. Unlike most young people, unused to speaking over a Public Address system, Paige noted, Ted held the microphone close to his lips, enunciating his words slowly and clearly to the crowd of mostly adolescents. He spoke of friendship and dedication and love that never dies, and basketball. It was mawkish and awful, but entirely heartfelt. She saw Glenn blink back a tear.

As he concluded his remarks, and blew the whistle to start the tournament, Paige noticed a smudge or something on Ted's right arm, just hidden by the sleeve of his tournament tee shirt. When he stepped back from the podium, she realized that what she had seen on Ted's arm was really a tattoo: OFW. For Oliver Frank Whiteside.

Paige was seized with a sudden urge to start giggling uncontrollably. She buried her head in Glenn's chest and snorted. Oh, dear, kind Ted. He was literally wearing Ollie on his sleeve, a permanent testament. How could she hate someone so unabashedly, awkwardly earnest? I'll bet a lot of girls ask him what the tattoo is for, Paige thought, which sent her into a fit of laughter. Glenn asked her if she felt alright, and her laughter continued, mixed with tears for Ollie, for herself, for her mother, for her husband. She rested her head on Glenn's shoulder as the tournament began. So, progress.

Paige and Roscoe arrived back at their house on the corner of Sixth and Chester. The dog skipped up the driveway, sniffing at the base of the basketball hoop that Glenn couldn't bear to take down yet. Maybe the next family that moves in here would like it, he had said. We won't be here forever. Paige unlocked the front door and Roscoe waddled inside.

"Come here, you old hound dog," Paige said to him, as she dug through her pocket for a dog treat, "Who's a good boy?"

10.   Being Alive

The nursery was yellow, with green gingham curtains. They'd painted it before Vivian was born, before they knew that Vivian would be Vivian and not Ben Junior. Yellow and green were nice, non-gender specific shades. The color trend, everyone said both in person and online, was taupe or brown or soft grey for nurseries these days, but Sally thought those were needlessly gloomy colors. A nursery ought to be a happy place, she thought. Ben agreed, but he really didn't care. He just wanted to keep Sally happy. Ben was wonderful.

Viv was now three and had graduated from the nursery to her own bedroom down the hall, painted a shade of peach that was bizarrely named "Flamingo Wing."

"I almost want to do the room a different color because of that stupid name," Ben had said. But it was a peaceful, sweet shade, and it matched their peaceful, sweet little peach of a toddler. Vivie was a strawberry blond, just like her Daddy, with a solemn face and wide blue eyes. She loved when Sally brushed and braided her hair. She sat quietly when Ben read her stories. At bedtime, she snuggled in with her stuffed bunny rabbit, Mr. Buns, and closed her eyes immediately.

"What are you going to dream about tonight, sweetie?" Sally would ask.

"Mommy and Daddy and Mr. Buns and Cawa," Vivie replied. Clara was her baby sister.

This time around, they knew that Clara would be Clara and not, once again, Ben Junior, but kept the nursey yellow. Shortly after Clara's arrival, Sally wished they had darkened the room because little Clara would not sleep.

"It doesn't really matter, does it?" asked Ben. "She doesn't sleep in the middle of the night when it's pitch black. It's not the color that's upsetting her."

It wasn't merely that the baby was awake. When Clara was awake, she screamed a throaty, cough-like scream that, to Sally, seemed hardly human.

"Viv never cried like that," Sally told her mother.

"All babies are different; you just got spoiled with Viv."

Sally's mother was right. Vivian's placidity had made Sally believe that all babies were docile and gentle. They had not been trying for a sibling yet, and Sally was surprised, but not too concerned, when she discovered she was pregnant. For one thing, she didn't have the terrible morning sickness that she had suffered from with Viv. Until her twenty-week ultrasound, both Sally and Ben had been convinced that this next baby was male, by virtue of how different everything felt. Ben had referred to Sally's belly as "Benjie" and "Little Bro" so convinced was he.

"Looks like baby's going to turn for us now. Mom and Dad, are you sure you want to know the sex?" said the technician.

"Yes!" they chimed in chorus, holding hands. And the blurry shaped on the screen rolled on its side and kicked its legs.

"And we've got ourselves a little girl!" she cried.

They'd been happy, of course, especially Sally, but they were floored. And as it turned out, Clara was nothing at all like Vivian. She had dark-hair and olive skin, like Sally, most decidedly not a little peach. Clara was not soft and docile. She fussed and scratched at her face with tiny talon-like fingernails.

Neither Ben nor Sally's mother could sooth her; she screamed and screamed till Sally lifted her up. She was constantly hungry.

Viv slept dutifully in the adjacent bedroom with her little rump in the air and clutching Buns by the ears. But with Clara, all bets were off. Sally was late to everything since Clara was born nineteen months ago; she was late to life. Because of Clara's constant, insistent neediness, Sally couldn't bounce back. She couldn't find the time to lose the baby weight because when Clara finally slept, Sally collapsed in an exhausted heap instead of scampering over to the Park District. She hadn't gotten the girls their Halloween costumes yet and all the cute ones would be sold out. Vivie wanted them to be Elsa and Anna from *Frozen*, which was adorable but Sally couldn't find an Elsa costume in 2T for Clara. Assuming, of course, that she would consent to wear it; Clara shrieked in protest of certain outfits, for no discernible reason.

The battles with Clara had started immediately. Sally couldn't even breastfeed Clara for more than three days. The infant had been relentless. Tiny, squirming Clara would not, could not, unlatch. Viv had been only a little over a year and a half when her sister arrived, and needed attention. Ben was helpless, trying to comfort Vivie, trying to get some sleep himself. And Clara would not stop nursing. When Sally pulled her away, Clara shrieked. By the time Sally took her first post-partum shower, she screamed in pain when the warm water hit her chest. And that was that; she gave up and mixed some formula. Clara, who didn't seem to care as long as Sally was holding her, sucked contentedly on her bottle.

Of course, then Sally felt guilty. But Sally admittedly felt guilty about everything. She felt guilty for compromising her baby's immune system by resorting to bottle-feeding. She felt guilty for not getting out enough with Viv. She felt guilty about not getting out enough for herself, thereby setting a poor example for both her daughters. She felt guilty for quitting her job at Meyers Forman Worth, LLP. She felt guilty for spending all that money to go to Law School, only to quit working when she got married. She felt guilty that her friend Lael was undergoing IVF, while Sally got pregnant instantaneously. She felt guilty that she didn't contribute to the family income. She felt guilty that Ben had to work so hard to support them. She felt guilty that she had gotten pregnant and Ben had felt compelled to marry her out of some latent Catholic remorse.

And all that was just the beginning. She hadn't even touched upon the way her house looked, though God knows, her mother did when she came to visit. That was always a sure bet. Sally's mother would tell her how "lucky" Sally was that she could stay home with her babies because most women didn't get that luxury, and wasn't she lucky that Ben wasn't the kind of man who demanded a fancy meal prepared every night, like Sally's father had wanted? Plus, Sally gets to live in a nice town like Whistler where there are parks she can take the girls to, not like the city, where Sally grew up. Sally just needed to bundle her girls up better or they were liable to catch a cold. And, honey, please don't take this wrong, but would it kill you to vacuum a little?

Clara started screaming whenever Sally turned on the vacuum cleaner, so she simply stopped vacuuming. The stovetop was coated with grease; dishes, pans and silverware littered the countertops and kitchen table, all in various degrees of crustiness. The family room floor was invisible under a thick layer of Vivie's Barbie dolls, stuffed animals, and plastic bananas, bunches of grapes and sirloin steaks from her play grocery cart.

It occurred to Sally that her children were running her life; she simply did not know how she could stop the process without making herself feel worse. Whenever she reprimanded three-year-old Viv, or let Clara 'cry it out," the resulting rush of self-doubt and remorse was paralyzing. Sally cried, and Clara cried, and Viv watched *Max and Ruby* cartoons over and over.

There was Cherry Tree, thank God. Cherry Tree Preschool, just seven minutes away in that beautiful building near Otis Pond. Viv went there Monday through Thursday mornings from nine to noon. And then Sally was alone with Clara, who slept. So naturally Sally, who had been up all night with Clara, slept. Which made her feel guilty that she wasn't cleaning the toilets or planning dinner or putting on a clean shirt.

Thanks to Cherry Tree Preschool, Sally had met her first real friend in Whistler, Martha Zeigler. Sally and Martha switched off days when they drove each other's children to preschool, allowing the other to rest. Sawyer, Martha's girl, was her youngest; the others were already in the elementary school on the other side of Bartleby Park. The women had worked out a system with old car seats that Martha's older children had outgrown. All they had to do was sign a waiver with Wendy, the head instructor over at Cherry Tree, authorizing the other as a designated drop-off and pick-up Parent, and voila: three hours of peace! It was rough on Sally when she had to pick up Sawyer at the Zeigler's, since she had to get both Clara and Viv bundled into the car, but Sally lived for the days when Martha took little Viv by the hand and toddled her off in her grey minivan.

"Hi there, Princess, how are you doing this morning?" Martha said to Viv.

"I'm good!" Vivie sang.

"Of course you are, Angel." She smiled. "Sawyer!" Martha barked to her own toddler, "Get whatever that is out of your mouth and sit still!" And Martha drove off, with Viv waving for the back car-seat.

Three hours till Martha would bring her back. Sally had three hours, if only Clara would nap. But Clara, distressingly, would not sleep. Sally held Clara in her lap and rocked her, singing "Puff the Magic Dragon" tonelessly, but Clara's dark eyes never closed. When Sally's rear end got tired, she tried putting Clara in the bouncy seat and then the swing, but Clara wriggled and whined against the safety restraints.

"Don't you want to sleep, Clarabelle?" she asked.

"Da!" smiled Clara and grabbed Sally's hair.

At ten-thirty or so, Sally started bundling them both up to go to the park. She changed Clara's diaper, prepared a bottle, assembled a packet of Cheerio snacks, dressed Clara in a warm onesie (the one with the ducklings on it), and her new plaid coat with the precious toggle-buttons on it. She couldn't find Clara's booties, so Sally grabbed a fleece blanket to drape over her. What else? A hat. It was getting colder and colder in the mornings now, despite the bright sunshine. Sally found one of Clara's old hats in the bins next to the front door. By the time Sally got Clara seated in the stroller, Clara had taken her hat off and thrown the blanket down. After a few more minutes' struggling, they were ready to leave.

"Key!" Clara cried as they were leaving the house. Kitty, Clara's favorite stuffed animal (that was actually a lemur, Ben once unsuccessfully tried to point out) was in Sally's diaper bag.

They proceeded down the driveway.

"Bee-Bee!" Clara cried.

"Sweetie, you don't need your Binky now; we're going to the park. You don't want to lose Binky or get Binky dirty, do you?"

The Bee-Bee, Binky or pacifier was a sticking point between Ben and Sally. Ben claimed that pacifiers ruined teeth, resulted in braces and generally contributed to global moral ruin. Sally believed they temporarily shut up her high-strung baby, and Sally was the one home with Clara, after all. There were, hence, Bee-Bees stashed in various corners of the Bundren household. But taking a pacifier out to the park was asking for trouble. Sally had slept maybe four hours last night and was in no mood to be extra vigilant regarding Bee-Bee's whereabouts. Nope, the Binky stayed at home.

But Clara screamed "Bee-Bee! Bee-Bee!" wailing so frantically that Sally was afraid old Mrs. Lundgren who lived next door might pull back her checked kitchen curtains and glare at her, like she had done last weekend after the unfortunate yogurt incident (don't ask). Clara actually sounded like someone had set her on fire or something. It was mortifying. Sally dug around for the house keys, which were probably buried somewhere in the bottom of the diaper bag, perhaps lodged under the Cheerios or the extra outfit Sally packed in case Clara had a blow-out or threw up all over herself or something.

"Bee-Bee, Mama!" wailed little Clara. Sally turned the stroller around to the garage, and typed in the code at the console on the side of the door. She must have messed something up because it didn't work the first time, but on the second try it opened slowly. She pushed Clara into the garage, wedged the stroller next to the Subaru Forester, and opened the door that led to the laundry room and the rest of the house. Now, where was the stupid Binky? After three comic circles around the first floor, Sally spotted a pacifier inside one of Viv's hot pink Crocs.

"Gotcha!" she muttered, brushing stray fuzzies and dirt off.

Clara was not, to Sally's great relief, wailing anymore. Instead, she was busily engaged in rubbing her tiny hands onto the Forester's filthy wheel-well. Sally rushed back inside for a wet-wipe, thankful that she had spotted the box when searching for Clara's Binky a moment ago. She cleaned Clara's fingers, amid squeals of protest, gave the child her binky, and then pushed the stroller out of the garage. They were off again. It was five blocks to Bartleby Park.

For such an upscale suburb as Whistler, you'd think they would take better care of the sidewalks, Sally thought to herself as she pushed Clara down Fremont Lane to Chester Street. She had to maneuver the stroller around cracks and holes, with Clara crying "Ba! Ba!" and giggling every time the wheels hit a bump.

As they turned onto Chester, and into the sunshine, Sally started to feel better. The cool breeze was refreshing, not chilling, and didn't the leaves look pretty? She pointed out the pretty colors to Clara ("Look, sweetie, a yellow leaf!" "And this one is brown!") as they passed the school, the parking lot, and finally found their way onto Bartleby Park. A few dog-walkers milled around the saucer shaped bottom of the field, causing Clara to squeal "Doggie woof!" and wave her hands excitedly. Sally steered the stroller towards the small playground area, enclosed on the west side of the park with a tasteful wrought iron fence.

"Ok, little Missy, how about a swing on the swings?" Sally asked, plucking Clara out of the stroller.

Alright, so maybe things weren't so terrible after all, Sally mused, as she pushed her beautiful little daughter on a swing in a beautiful park on a beautiful morning in, admittedly, a beautiful town. Viv was at Cherry Tree till around twelve-fifteen, and Sally would have a chance to chat with Martha for a few minutes when she dropped Viv off. That would be fun. Martha didn't get all bogged down with things; she was a pro – she had two older kids going to Washington Elementary School. All day! They didn't even come home for lunch! Motherhood seemed so effortless and off the cuff with Martha, who could be delightfully snarky about some of the mothers at Washington. It would be another year and half till Viv went to Kindergarten. At least then, Clara would be old enough for Cherry Tree herself. Imagine how that could feel, having actual time alone.

"How's that, baby girl, all done?" Sally asked.

"Ah dah!" replied Clara.

This was motherhood, Sally thought. This is what you work for. A house in the suburbs, a gorgeous husband, so what if he has to work so hard that he's never home, and they want him to start travelling -- his salary will go up. You make sacrifices; you're an adult. You have two tiny people who depend on you now. It was better than poring over box after box of discovery documents at ole Meyers Foreman Worth.

"LLP," Sally added aloud.

Sally had adored law school, and did well. She had made Law Review, and wrote for the Journal of Health Law, as well as the Women's Law Journal. She competed on the school's Moot Court team and worked as a Teaching Assistant for Legal Writing in her third and final year. She longed to clerk for a Federal Judge, but her grades weren't nearly high enough and her law school wasn't quite prestigious enough. They were, however, enough to open doors for Sally to interview at some

"Big Law" firms in the city, with their offices spanning six to ten floors of glass skyscrapers, offering dizzying views and dizzying salaries.

An offer came from Meyers Foreman Worth LLP. Sally had been attracted to the firm for its strong Antitrust Law division. Every young attorney longed to be involved in a big juicy Antitrust case, but Sally was placed in Commercial Litigation department, and spent her first two year as MFW in a windowless room lined with bankers boxes, where she and two other newly-hatched associates pored over ten thousand pages of documents produced in response to Interrogatories, and pulling out those that might be considered privileged by their client, a multinational bank being accused of stealing trade secrets from small tech start-up company.

Junior Associates were paired with seasoned attorneys as their mentors. Sally's was Greg Leatham, a Partner at Meyers Foreman, specializing in Insurance Defense cases. She accompanied Greg to State and Federal Courts, learned how to draft Motions to Dismiss, depose witnesses and argue for Summary Judgment. Unlike the unabashedly hostile, or the less overt paternalistic and condescending treatment many of the new female attorneys received from their male counterparts, Greg was always courteous and patient with Sally. He saw to it that she stopped spending valuable time doing mind-numbing document reviews, and gave Sally engrossing legal research projects. Sure, Insurance Defense wasn't glamorous, and sure, making legal findings that claims should be denied could be brutal, but they provided a service for their clients. And a client is a client, whether it be State Farm and MetLife or John Q. Public. Greg was a quick and thoughtful lawyer, smooth with clients and fair with adversaries. He was a second father to Sally.

Roughly a year after Sally started her tenure at Meyers Foreman, Greg Leatham was quite literally gone overnight. The firm's Chair, Max Reiner, sent out an email announcement that Greg had retired. His open cases were all redistributed among the other Insurance Defense partners. Over the course of the next few days, Sally gleaned what had transpired from other lawyers, paralegals and docket clerks. Greg had been brought before an emergency Equity Partners Meeting for an incident regarding Greg, his cell phone and the Ladies bathroom on the forty-second floor.

Sally was aghast. The sensational story was retold throughout the firm. Sally even enjoyed a brief period of mini-celebrity, as mentee to the disgraced Greg. Nobody believed Sally's protestations of ignorance, thinking her vacuously blinded by loyalty. Sally herself wondered how any of this was possible. Law firms and lawyering were fundamentally messed up, she concluded, especially Insurance Defense, screwing over poor slobs with technicalities in the fine print. It was all smoke and mirrors and phony posturing. Even Greg Leatham, Jesus. She longed to change careers, but didn't know how to start.

During her third year as an attorney that Sally was introduced to Ben Bundren at a Friday Happy Hour at The Exchequer Pub in the city. Ben was not a lawyer, but knew several of her colleagues. He worked as a financial advisor for high net worth clients. About six years Sally's senior, Ben had a sharp nose and jaw, with unruly strawberry blond hair. More importantly, Ben also had a sharp and ribald sense of humor that shocked Sally into snorts of laughter at their first meeting. They exchanged numbers that evening and started to date.

Sally realized she was pregnant about five months into their relationship. Once again, she was blindsided by something that was simply not supposed to happen. She was on the pill. She took them at the right time all the time. Didn't she?

Sally waited three days before telling Ben, shaking and crying into her hands so that he wouldn't see her face. Gallant Ben put his arms around Sally.

"Ok, honey, ok, Sal. Why don't you marry me then?"

He got her the stunner of a ring later: two carats. They were married at Sally's childhood parish, Our Lady of Charity, because the only thing Sally's parents disliked more than a pregnant bride was a civil service at some County Building. In a blur of morning sickness and euphoria, Sally quit her job at Meyers Foreman Worth ("LLP"), moved in with her new husband, had a baby ("Vivian Marie, 8 pounds, 3 ounces") and started looking for a home in the suburbs. Before long, they were cozily ensconced on charming Fremont Lane in sought-after Whistler.

Sally's attorney friends told her they were jealous of her life. "I mean, look at him!" said Jamie, "Who wouldn't want *that* guy coming home to you?"

"And oh my goodness, you're going to be the cutest little mommy!" squealed Piper. "And you'll be living in Pleasantville!" The associates at Meyers Foreman presented Sally with a joint Baby Shower Farewell party. Sally sipped San Pellegrino and tried to keep the cake down.

Motherhood terrified and thrilled and isolated Sally. She had horrible fantasies of dropping little Vivian on the tile floor of their beautiful new sunroom. She rocked her little peach and sang to her, with tears that she really didn't understand dripping down off her nose and onto the baby's blanket.

"If you'll be M-I-N-E mine
I'll be T-H-I-N-E thine,
And I'll L-O-V-E love you
All the T-I-M-E tine.
You are the B-E-S-T best
Of all the R-E-S-T rest
And I'll L-O-V-E love you
All the T-I-M-E time."

And Vivie fell perfectly asleep.

Sally was suddenly supposed to be an expert, as if, by virtue of having given birth, you gained some mystical, secret knowledge. But the reality of her situation was: she was alone, alone, alone. Sally would screw it up; Vivian would be ruined forever. But Vivian was so quiet and amazing and sweet; Sally must be doing something right, right?

And then came Clara. Furious, fuzzy little Clara, the baby she'd gotten pregnant with way too soon because she'd heard you wouldn't get pregnant if you were breastfeeding. Sally's obstetrician, Mia, had laughed merrily at that story.

"I get a lot of those," she said. "You'd be surprised."

Ben, being Ben, gave his best Jeff Goldblum imitation: "Life, uh, life finds a way." he deadpanned, while Sally held little Viv and tried to wrap her brain around doing it all over again.

They had been married over three years now. Her family was beautiful. Her home was beautiful. Her life was beautiful. She lived in Whistler, for crying out loud! Do you know how much their brick house on Fremont Lane had cost? Back in the city, her former colleagues were arguing over whether their adversary's Complaint should be dismissed on a 2-615 Motion or a 2-619 Motion, but Sally got to take her little girl to a park and watch her play.

Sally placed little Clara back into the stroller and clicked the seatbelt. She needed to get lunch ready for Vivie, who would generally only eat chicken nuggets shaped like dinosaurs. Maybe some applesauce and macaroni for Clara. The back of Sally's head suddenly started to throb; her sleepless night was catching up with her. The distance back to Fremont Lane seemed to lengthen.

"Ba!" sang Clara, "Ba!" as Sally pushed her over the sidewalks' bumps. They passed a neat little house where a vigorous, grey-haired lady raked leaves. She had narrow red glasses on her face and another pair on top of her head. She wore a green wool sweater, with oak leaves sticking to her back and elbows -- from how hard she's raking, Sally thought as she and Clara went by.

"Morning," said the woman.

"Good morning!" Sally replied brightly. What a friendly town this was, after all.

Without any warning, Clara started to scream.

"Bee-Bee!" she shrieked over and over. "Bee-Bee!"

Sally stopped the stroller. "Oh, Clara, did you drop your Binky?" Sally searched under the fleece blanket, in the folds of

Clara's coat, even under her daughter's little rump, but found nothing. Clara kept screaming. The old woman paused in her raking.

"You must have thrown it out in the park," Sally told her. She could feel the woman staring at her from behind. "We'll go home super-duper quick and get you another one!"

"Bee-Bee!" Clara was red-faced and inconsolable.

Sally crouched down in front of the stroller and stared Clara in the face. "Listen, Kiddo. I didn't want to bring the stupid Binky in the first place. You're the one who dropped it. Now shut up and let me get you home." She hissed, and started pushing the stroller.

Clara was shocked speechless for a few seconds, and then let out a wail. She seemed not even to need to inhale to keep her continuous noise going. Too afraid to look at the old woman with the rake, who was doubtless scandalized by her behavior, Sally breathed deep and continued pushing the stroller down Chester Street, past Sixth and onto Fremont Lane. Clara screamed and screamed as they passed over every crack and hole in the sidewalk. When they arrived at home, Sally found the house-keys in her jacket pocket, where they had been all along, and let them in.

Clara had screeched herself into a fitful doze. Her face was pink and tear-stained. Sally checked the time, 11:30. She had just enough time to catch a little nap before Martha dropped Vivie off. Forget cooking the dinosaur nuggets; maybe they'd drive up Route 40 and go to McDonalds for lunch. They could get Happy Meals; Clara could get a yogurt and fruit parfait or maybe even a sundae for dessert and make a mess; Sally could eat French fries and have a Coke. The girls would love it and Sally would be a hero, not a slacker. She *was* a good mother.

Sally parked Clara and her stroller in a sunbeam next to the sofa and laid down on it. Her shoulders ached; her eye sockets felt swollen. When would she be able to get just a few solid hours of decent rest? What was she going to make for dinner? When was she going to start preparing for the holidays?

135

Why did she tell everyone they would host Thanksgiving? Ben wanted to badly for everyone to see the perfect little family they'd built out here in Whistler. Maybe they could cater because there was no way on God's green earth she could pull off a major holiday. Sally drifted off.

The refrigerator hummed softly in the next room. A passing flock of Canadian geese honked high above the house on Fremont Lane. Sally's phone buzzed with a text notification, jolting her awake. Her hair was askew and there was a small circle drool puddled on the cuff of her shirtsleeve where Sally had rested her head while dozing. It was 12:05; Martha would be dropping Vivian off any minute. Great, she hadn't even washed the dishes. She'd had three hours; couldn't she at least have showered? Martha was going to see that not one thing in her disaster-area kitchen had been altered since this morning.

She was a failure as a parent. If she couldn't get this stuff done right, how on earth could she be expected to raise these girls to be women? Someday Ben was going to figure out that she was terrible at this whole motherhood thing and he would just leave her and he would be right. He would tell Sally that she was pathetically inept, starting with the way she'd blundered into getting pregnant – both times -- to the half-assed way she was currently raising their daughters. What was the point of this all? She looked down at the baby, slumped down in the stroller next to her.

Clara opened her eyes, looked up at Sally, and smiled.

Acknowledgements

Deepest gratitude to my husband, Bob, and our children, Owen and Nora, my *sine qua non*. Your constant love and support made this book both possible and worthwhile.

84005025R00081

Made in the USA
Lexington, KY
18 March 2018